LAD

Aber		Lyi	
Bel	4/93	Mc	
C.C.		M.	
C.P.	4/95	Ot.	
Dick		P.N.	
Elm		P.S.	
G.S.A.		P.P.	
Mt.Pl.		St.A.	
Sgt.		St.J.	6/06
Gen		S.L.	
G.V.		Ven	
G.H.		Vets	3/02
Har	9/93	T.T.	2/96, 2/05
Jub		NLm	12/98

Bev		S.C	
Emm		T.M.	
G.S.P.		V.P.	11/04, 6/05 Knper
P.C.P.		W.L.	
P.M.		S.M.	
W.L.			Reynolds 2/97
Q.A.			KL 6/01 (Macklin) 2/05
	MB 5/00		Henderson 7/05
	Beaudry 12/02		St.M 3/07

THE
DEVIL'S
BOUNTY

This Large Print Book carries the
Seal of Approval of N.A.V.H.

THE
DEVIL'S
BOUNTY

LARRY JAY MARTIN

Thorndike Press • Thorndike, Maine

Library of Congress Cataloging in Publication Data:

Martin, Larry Jay.
  The devil's bounty / by Larry Jay Martin.
    p. cm.
  ISBN 1-56054-480-5 (alk. paper : lg. print)
  1. Large type books.   I. Title.
[PS3563.A72487D48   1992]   92-18699
813'.54—dc20   CIP

Thorndike Press Large Print edition published in 1992
by arrangement with Bantam Books, a division of
Bantam Doubleday Dell Publishing Group, Inc.

Cover design by Studio 3.

The tree indicium is a trademark of Thorndike Press.

This book is printed on acid-free, high opacity paper. ⊛

For my brother,
REX L. MARTIN
who had to be much more
than that

CHAPTER ONE

From the deep shadows of a ravine bracketed by river willows, four robed men — strangers to this quiet riverside — watched in sullen silence. At the sound of approaching hoofbeats they hunkered down, hidden by the cleft's edge, and waited.

Beneath a towering gnarled cottonwood, Apolonia Vega drew rein on her sorrel stallion, tossed her long coal-black tresses out of her eyes, and watched the hundred-fifty-foot steamer *Senator* churning up the wide Sacramento on its way to the newly platted city of the same name. Voices floated across the water singing to the tune of the popular "Oh, Susanna" that she had heard so much in the last year. The singers were accompanied by two amateur instrumentalists perched in the midst of piles of cargo on a large bail of hemp rope, fiddle and flute in hand.

I came from Salem City,
  With my washboard on my knee,
I'm going to California,
  The gold dust for to see.
It rained all night the day I left,
  The weather it was dry,
The sun so hot I froze to death,
  Oh brothers don't you cry.

The voices began to fade as the steamer drew near and the men realized that a beautiful señorita sat astride a handsome tall stallion watching their progress.

Men crossed the boat from the far side and a group of men five deep in slouch hats, brown canvas pants, red and blue woolen shirts, and knee-high hobnail boots, with picks and shovels and packs, crowded the portside rail. In almost reverent silence, as even the flute and fiddle players had stopped to stare, they waved to her. She stole a glance over her shoulder up to the road forty paces behind and above her and saw that her *dueña,* her chaperon, Tomasa Madariaga, was engaged in lively conversation with the old vaquero, José Romero, who drove the buggy.

Apolonia carefully returned the wave, her hand concealed from those who watched over her. A foot-stomping cheer arose from the festive mass of gold hunters.

Across the fifty yards of water separating the shore from the double-decked steamship, barn swallows dipped and dove. They, too, seemed to revel in the simple exchange of people so close in distance, yet so far apart in culture. A regal blue heron winged overhead with the aplomb the California señorita was expected to observe in this situation.

Apolonia smiled for the first time that afternoon.

With even more exuberance the song resumed.

Oh! California,
   That's the land for me,
I'm going to Sacramento,
   With my washboard on my knee.

She had seen many such men pass over her father's rancho on foot and on horseback, and many more filled large boats to the rails and small boats to the point of swamping, heading for the gold fields.

She had seen almost as many return, half starved, dejected.

But there were a few who had hit it big, and Sacramento City and the recently renamed city of San Francisco grew by leaps and bounds as a result of stories told and retold, growing in splendor with each telling — streets paved with gold, nuggets for the taking. She remembered eight years ago, as a young girl of ten, visiting Yerba Buena — now booming San Francisco, but then little more than the squat Mission Dolores and a few huts among sand hills, reached by slopping across the wide mud flats at low tide, or small boats at high. It was said the city was now twenty-five thousand strong, a mass of men and tents and clapboard buildings that filled every square foot. On one patch of public land south of the city, facetiously known as Happy Valley, over a thousand tents of cotton duck and rubber, known to the miners as Mr. Goodyear's finest, swelled out of the earth like a mass of pointed blisters.

The *Senator* blew its mournful whistle, rounding the bend in the distance. The exuberant voices and the thumping of the steam pistons disappeared, and Apolonia nudged the stallion on down the riverside trail, enjoying the afternoon sunshine, though she knew she should not.

Her father had forbidden her to take her usual afternoon ride, and for the first time she could remember she had willfully disobeyed him. Had her chaperons, Tomasa and José, known of his edict they would never have allowed her to ride away from the hacienda. She had been careful not to let them see her

10

anger or hear of his.

Glancing up at the afternoon sun, she wondered if it was four o'clock yet. If so, Gaspar Cota, the reason she had disobeyed her father, would be arriving at the hacienda of Rancho del Rio Ancho. Her father would even now be sending one of the Indian serving women to find her, and when her absence was discovered, he would fume in anger.

Apolonia bent low in the saddle to make her way under a dense thatch of overhanging river willows, her tight black riding jacket biting into her stomach. Clearing the branches, she straightened and smoothed the long velvet-trimmed skirt that demurely hid her ankles and most of the leather *tapaderos* protecting the saddle's carved wooden stirrups.

She sighed deeply, wondering if she had the slightest chance of dissuading her father from his plans. Then she set her jaw with determination. She would not marry the pompous ass Gaspar Cota, a man almost twice her age. A man whom she detested. She would not!

She raised her arm to fend off the river growth, encouraging the stallion into a shadowed cleft where the willows were the thickest. She gasped as strong hands encircled her waist and she was suddenly jerked from the saddle. She tried to scream, but the ground

11

rushed up and her breath was expelled by the slamming blow to the trail.

Her eyes swam; she fought for air. Masked faces! Powerful hands pinned her to the sandy trail, then hauled her to her feet.

She gagged and fought the callused hand covering her mouth. Her eyes flared, her view filled with brown teeth behind a soup-strainer mustache, and the laughing face of a man looming in front of her — dressed in Chinese robes. He held a cloth bag, reaching to put it over her head while unseen hands pinned her arms to her sides.

With a rush of strength, she kicked out and buried her pointed high-top shoe in the burly man's crotch.

"Aiee, ye bitch!" he screamed.

Apolonia clamped her teeth into the rough palm covering her mouth and got the salty taste of blood before the hand jerked free. She realized the man with the cloth bag had cold blue eyes the instant before he snarled and dropped the sack into place over her head.

She struggled against her bindings and the fear of darkness, managing a muffled scream. Then the cloth was bound tightly around her mouth.

She felt herself being hauled up and winced when her stomach slammed across the saddle. She struggled against the tight, suffocating ropes and gag, and bile choked her. She was afraid she would vomit, which would have been life-threatening with her mouth bound. Trying to calm herself, she began silently to pray.

"Apolonia!" a nearby gruff voice rang out. José — it was old José! He would make them stop.

She jerked away as a pistol roared near her ear. Then the horse bucked with a bone-jarring dance and she was almost thrown from the saddle. To her relief, the animal quieted — but she could feel its shivers through the saddle and wished she could comfort the horse with a stroke on the neck or a quiet word. Strong hands shoved her roughly back up-right.

Apolonia, her ears still ringing from the blast, heard a low moan, and despair flooded her — for herself, and more so for old José. Even through the cloth, the acrid odor of gun smoke seared her nostrils.

With its rider bound tightly to the saddle, the horse was led away. Apolonia began to sob, but quickly quieted, steeling her resolve not to show these barbarians any weakness. *Pray, Apolonia, do not cry.* In the distance she heard the shouts of her *dueña*, but they faded, as did the moans of her old friend, her father's trusted vaquero.

The horse's hooves sucked at mud, then finally quieted, and she heard the men dismount. Her knowledge of English was good enough that she understood the gruff voice instructing her as she was jerked from the horse, placed on her feet, and made to walk.

"Don't ye be fightin', now, me pretty Polly. Ye best get used to it. It's a long, long trip for ye." The voice didn't waver as strong hands hoisted her easily, then deposited her against the hard wooden ribs of what she knew must be a small boat. Waves lapped at the sides and she heard the boat scrape against the bottom, then felt it levitate away from a muddy shore. It rocked violently to the side as others clamored in and jostled her roughly with knees and backsides when they took their places on the thwarts.

The oars clattered into place and began to dip in a steady rhythm. One of the oarsmen whistled a lively tune, grating her shattered nerves. She struggled against her bonds, and faith waned. With each stroke she was farther and farther from Rancho del Rio Ancho. The bilge water in the bottom of the boat soaked through her clothes and she shuddered, but not from the cold.

She wished she had obeyed her father.

CHAPTER TWO

John Clinton Ryan sat astride his palomino stallion, Diablo, one long leg hooked over the pommel, his wide-brimmed hat pushed back on his head, exposing a shock of sandy hair.

Behind him on Front Street men hustled in every direction — afoot, horseback, and in every possible horse-drawn contraption, including a fire wagon that careened by with bells clanging and buckets banging and men hanging on desperately to its wooden sides. He admired the four matched grays that pulled it, as well as the kelly green brass-trimmed wagon with the yellow words MONUMENTAL FIRE COMPANY painted boldly along the length. San Francisco had already burned twice this year.

But it was the sight that stretched before him that caused his real wonder. More than eight hundred ships — a winter forest of barren masts — covered the bay beyond the tide-out mud flats. Even more wondrous was the sight of two corpses, heads grotesquely canted, tongues distended, swaying with the quiet roll of the ship from the yardarm of a sixty-cannon U.S. frigate moored not more than a cable's length from shore. Examples, he had been told. Left hanging to discourage the rest of the crew from deserting and following the thousands of others who had left their ships to the watery graveyard the bay had become.

Clint Ryan had had his years at sea, and her cruelties were usually no surprise to him. But for the U.S. Navy to leave two of her own to be picked at by the seabirds and stared at by throngs of Chileans, Chinese, Australians, Sandwich Islanders, and thousands of others from every nook and cranny and filthy crevice of the earth's ends? His mouth dried and his brow furrowed at the sight of it.

Reining the big stallion away, Clint urged the powerful animal into the milling throng on Front Street. Little puffs of dust led the way as they plodded through the hock-deep powder, passing tents and clapboard shops, weaving through horsebackers and wagons laden with freight. It was not the California Clint was used to. No lethargy here, no *poco tiempo,* no *mañana.* These men were going somewhere, each with a determined stride,

16

each with a set to his jaw and a gleam of hope in his eye.

Clint drew rein and glanced at the long, permanent wooden building in front of him. It stretched along the street for well over a hundred feet. Glass, in several huge three-by-six-foot panes, covered the length and advertised to those on the street the longest bar in San Francisco. A year ago a two-by-two panel of glass was a rarity in California. Clint looked above the amazing wall of glass and read the garish sign, THE EL DORADO SALOON, in bold two-foot gilded letters.

He had been most of a month on the trail, El Camino Real, traveling from the sleepy pueblo of Los Angeles up the coast to Santa Barbara, where he spent some time with friends. Then he had gone on to see for himself what he had heard was happening in San Francisco.

Clint had originally come to California because it was his job. A sailor went wherever the ship he was currently signed on went. But she ran aground and broached, and he found himself a resident. At first his mind was set on getting back at sea, but being blamed for the wreck of the *Savannah* had changed all that.

Three years in California had given him a new hope, a life on the land, a life as a landowner. The upheaval and political change in California during those three years made any planning speculative at best. But during a trip deep into the Ton Tache Valley, as the large central valley of California was known to the Mexicans and Indians, he had solidified his hopes. On the banks of the river called Kaweah lay a beautiful live-oak-covered, river- and stream-fed rancho. A fertile land, home to elk and deer and wildfowl of all kinds. With grass belly deep and rich. Land suited for the raising of cattle and horses. Land claimed only by the Yocuts Indians, and he had already made his peace with them. Now the problem was garnering title, making the land — the dream — his.

It had been a long trip up El Camino Real and Clint ran his tongue over gritty teeth. He was dry as dirt.

Reining the stallion to a rail that he recognized as the purloined boom of a ship, he shouldered the palomino between a bay and a dappled gray. He dismounted, loosened the palomino's cinch, untied his saddlebags and draped them over his shoulder, pulled the revolving breech Colt rifle from its scabbard, and started for the batwing doors that welcomed all comers to the noisy saloon.

Assailed by the odor of tobacco smoke, sweat, and dirt, he crowded between men of all sizes, colors, and descriptions. There were Peruvians in wide flat-brimmed hats with tassels bobbing from the rim, Chinese in robes with long queues hanging to their waists, Chileans in hats like upside down bean pots half hiding dark-skinned faces, which rose out of slitted wide-striped ponchos. Californios, dressed as Clint was in embroidered jackets and *calzonevas* with flat or slouch hats, carried reatas even into the saloon. In addition to foreigners, the room teemed with men from every corner of the United States and her territories — most of them sporting hobnailed boots with their canvas pants tucked in and flannel shirts covering long johns. Each had at least a knife at his waist and many had hatchets on their belts to boot. Most had one pistol, and some a pair, shoved into their belts. A few, like Clint, carried rifles or shotguns as well. All looked as if they were more than proficient with the weapons they toted. And the weapons appeared to be needed: More gold covered the fifty round wooden tables, where men drank or gambled with dice and cards, than Clint had expected to see in a lifetime.

Shouldering his way between two miners clad in red shirts, canvas pants, and brogans, Clint bellied up to the bar and leaned his Colt's rifle against it. Six bartenders, big enough to handle beer kegs with ease, were stationed along the bar at twenty-foot intervals. They hoisted whiskey bottles and drew foaming mugs of beer. Mirrors as tall as the glass panels out front lined the intricately carved backbar, spaced between mahogany columns topped with sculptured gargoyles who glared down with evil relish through clouds of tobacco smoke at the crowded mass of sweaty men.

More bottles of liquor graced the backbar than Clint had seen in all the saloons from Mystic around the Horn to California. Maybe more than he had seen in all the ports he had called on in his twelve years at sea.

Champagne, Holland gin, sauterne, peach brandy, and whiskey in bottles of every size and description perched on multilayered shelves up to the ceiling and stood six deep on the backbar. Ale kegs in twenty different varieties hunkered under the brass-trimmed forebar. Labels in languages Clint couldn't read invited him to become lost in their elixir.

Suddenly the saloon quieted, as if a blanket of silence had been laid across it. Clint turned to see what the attraction was. Half a head taller than most of the men in the room, he could easily see why the deference was paid to the beautiful golden-haired woman who had entered through the batwing doors. Her Jenny Lind parasol, which perfectly matched her emerald green gown, twirled as the crowd parted to allow her to pass. In a wave from those by the door down the hundred-foot length of the bar, hats were snatched from heads. In the sudden silence, her laughter tinkled like silver bells as she crossed the room and disappeared up a short stairway near a small curtain-covered stage.

Dogging her steps, hat in hand, revealing his shining bald head, a man followed her closely. His eyes worked the room, taking note of any threat. As the curtains closed behind them, the room resumed its raucous roar. Clint overheard the word *sultry* and wondered if it was a description or a name.

Clint realized she was the first woman he had seen since he entered the city earlier in the day, and the first sunlight blond he had seen since he'd arrived in California years before.

Yes, San Francisco had changed in the three years since he had visited the quiet town of Yerba Buena while serving on board the brig *Savannah*.

That had been before the revolution, before the Treaty of Guadalupe Hidalgo, when the hide, horn, and tallow brig had struck a reef off Pt. Concepción, broached, and sunk with the loss of fourteen hands — men Clint had sailed around the Horn with. Quade Sharpentier, her captain, had made a formal accusation of Clint's malfeasance. But Clint was not at fault. He'd been below, asleep after twenty-four hours on duty, so he had been made the scapegoat by her captain. A U.S. warrant still existed for his arrest, he was sure, but he was unconcerned, as the thousands of men in San Francisco had something else on their minds. Gold.

And its glitter paled all other concerns.

The bartender stood across the bar, a knotty-faced man without eyebrows who looked as if he were first cousin to a bulldog and who wore the same disdainful expression as his brother gargoyles above.

"Well, mister, you drinkin' or leanin'?"

Clint's eyes narrowed, but he decided a drink was more important than trading insults or blows with an overworked bulldog bartender.

"Drinkin'. Give me a whiskey."

"I got fifty-four kinds of whiskey, emigrant, and twenty-five varieties of ale, and I ain't got no time to educate you. What'll it be?"

Clint leaned a little closer to the man, and his eyes hardened. "The closest kind."

The man's lip curled in a half smile. He reached for a bottle of Noble's Finest and up-ended it until the shot glass filled exactly to the ounce line. Holding the glass out of Clint's reach, he snarled, "Half a dollar."

"Half a dollar?" Clint grumbled in surprise.

"Same price as every saloon in San Fran, emigrant."

Clint dug into his pocket and tossed a handful of silver pesos clattering onto the bar.

"You best get to the diggin's, emigrant, and get you a satchel fulla gold. Boss don't like me takin' this greaser money." He paused as he eyed the money and Clint. "How come a Boston-talkin' man's a-wearin' those fancy Mexican duds?"

Clint didn't give the question the respect of an answer, just reached over and took the shot glass out of the man's hand, held it to his lips with relish, and upended it.

"Another?" the bartender asked. His mouth curled with the smirk-grin. "Or would you rather try the local swill?"

"How much for *aguardiente?*"

"Two bits."

"That'll do."

The bulldog bartender bent and pulled a clay bottle from under the bar, removed its carved pine plug with his teeth, and poured Clint another shot in the same glass. Clint dropped the coins on the bar and the man swiped them into his palm, then moved to another customer.

A few feet from Clint, a voice rang a mite

louder than the others in the bar. "An' that's so much horse dung."

Clint turned to his left and immediately spotted the two men, who were arguing nose to nose. A man leaning on the bar between Clint and the two picked up his glass and discreetly moved away. The one with his back to Clint stood straight and stiff, dressed in a smartly tailored black swallowtail coat and matching pants with a narrow-brimmed city high hat — the only one in the room. His boots shone with a bootblack's gleam, and he leaned on a gold-handled walking stick. The other man, of an equal height with the dude but with an ample girth, sported homespun clothes and a slouch hat, and his red shirt was splattered with tobacco juice — but he gave no quarter to the better-dressed man. He glared, his red face whiskey-blotched from too much time holding up the bar.

The man spat a stream of tobacco juice, missed the cuspidor, and backhanded the dribble from his chin. "Louisiana's Senator Soule is a no-account, and all he's doin' is gummin' up the works." Homespun glowered at High-hat and backed up a step as others moved away and gave the two more room.

"No-account?" High-hat repeated in a distinctly French accent. "M'sieur Soule has served Louisiana with honor, and it is M'sieur

24

Daniel Webster and M'sieur Seward who continue to keep California out of the Union."

"No, my frog friend" — Homespun's voice rose, and the crowded saloon began to quiet — "you and your kind not wantin' another free state is what's keepin' us out." Others in the crowd jeered at the Frenchman in agreement.

"Slavery is not the issue here," the Frenchman countered, his walking stick pounding in anger on the board floor. "We, too, want California in the Union. She is the gateway to the Pacific, to China, the Japans, and Hindustan, the fulfillment of our destiny as a great nation —"

"As long as you slavers keep men in chains and the planters have all the money," Homespun interrupted, "this country will never be worth a fiddler's length of gut."

Some of the crowd stirred in anger with this slight on the Union. Homespun rested his hand on the butt of the small cap-and-ball Root Patent Model pistol shoved into his belt next to a foot-long, leather-sheathed Arkansas toothpick.

But the Louisiana Frenchman was not deterred. "We abide by the law, M'sieur, as educated men should. Money follows those who toil with honor and use their God-given wits. And the law allows the ownership of slaves to help with that toil."

"Evil is evil, frog. Keepin' men like dogs and hoggin' all the money in the country is evil."

A man as large as Homespun stepped out of the crowd in between the two. He turned to face High-hat, his face nearly as black as the Frenchman's city suit. "We bes' be gettin' on now, Massa LaMont."

"Stand aside, Gideon."

"But Massa —"

"Aside, Gideon."

"Yessa," the black man said, but his eyes pleaded.

The Frenchman lifted his walking stick and shook it in Homespun's whiskey-blotched face. "Ignorant men such as yourself do not understand the economics of this great country and should not sully her name."

"Ignorant?" Homespun started to step forward, but the bulldog bartender swung the stubby double barrels of a scattergun across the bar.

"Outside, Vester Grumbles. You, too, Frenchy, or I'll blow you there."

Both men cut their eyes at the bartender and saw dogged determination.

"Sure as I'm Luther Baggs," the bartender said, lifting one hairless eyebrow, "I'll cut you in half." He motioned to the batwing doors with the scattergun. The saloon crowd faded back as if he were shaking the tail of a venom-spitting eight-foot timber rattler.

The Frenchman was the first to move, brushing past the man the bartender had called Grumbles, and the crowd parted. "I will be pleased to take my satisfaction outside, with pistols or fists," he said loud enough so all could hear. But if he carried a pistol, it was well concealed.

He was ten feet away when the glowering Grumbles came to life, jerking his Root and leveling it on the Frenchman's back as the hammer ratcheted.

Clint brought the heavy stock of his revolving breech rifle up in a sweeping motion, cracking Grumbles's forearm and knocking it upward. The Root's spat flame and smoke with a resounding blast that rocked the saloon but harmlessly holed the sculptured lead ceiling. Before Clint could close with the man, the black was on him. Two massive blows smashed Vester Grumbles, snapping his neck back and crumpling him to the foot of the bar. His head cracked soundly on the brass footrail, his arms splayed, sending a spittoon spinning and its contents of cigar butts, tobacco juice, and spittle flowing. Then he lay unmoving among soaked sawdust and peanut shells.

The Frenchman's look went from shock to

revulsion. "I should have known he was a coward."

Fear reflecting in the large brown eyes in his otherwise stoic face, the black glanced from man to man in the crowd, trying to weigh their thoughts. His gaze centered pleadingly on the man he had called master.

"I surely sorry, Massa," he mumbled, mostly for the benefit of the crowd, fearing he was about to be set upon and hanged from the nearest rafter, or whipped until dead — as he would have been for striking a white man in Louisiana.

With a booted foot, Clint toed the Root pistol aside and out of Grumbles's reach, just in case he awoke soon, but his face was already darkening with a massive blue lump the size of Gideon's fist, and he looked like he was out for some time.

The Frenchman moved closer to Gideon, his walking stick in one hand, the fancy gold handle shaking in the slave's face. "You know better than to raise your hands to a white man." The Frenchman's voice rang cold and aloof.

"I know, Massa LaMont, but —"

"Never again, Gideon. Never again, or I'll take the cane to you." He raised the walking stick threateningly.

Clint's jaw knotted with this change in events.

"Yessa," Gideon mumbled, and his gaze sank to the floor.

"That's the damnedest thing I ever heard," Clint managed, and some of the men in the crowd echoed his sentiment.

"Sir?" The Frenchman fixed his eyes on the newcomer.

"He knocked the gun aside, Massa," Gideon said quietly.

The Frenchman hesitated a moment. "I guess I owe you an imbibement, M'sieur, but we'll not discuss the discipline of my man, which is my business alone."

"Let me see, here," Clint said, studying the well-dressed man. "You owe me a drink, but you berate this man who saved your life sure as the sun rises in the east? That Root carries four more shots."

The Louisiana Frenchman puffed up and threw his shoulders back. "Do you desire the drink, M'sieur?"

"Soon as you thank this man and offer him something other than that fancy crutch across his back." He motioned to the big black man, who shook his head as if trying his best to silence Clint.

"This man is my property. It is his responsibility to protect my life —"

"Not in California, not to my way of thinking. Here a man steps up or stays out . . .

his choice." Those nearby clamored in both agreement and disagreement.

"I told you to take it outside," Baggs snapped. He motioned toward the batwing doors with his scattergun. "You, too, emigrant." He locked gazes with Clint.

Clint shrugged his shoulders, reached over and upended his *aguardiente,* then headed to the door. The crowd parted, making way.

Deciding he had had enough of the El Dorado and saloons for one day, Clint moved straight to his horse. He shoved the rifle into its saddle scabbard, cinched the big palomino tightly, and mounted just as the doors swung away and the Frenchman, followed closely by his slave, stepped through. From behind, where the Frenchman couldn't see, Gideon nodded and flashed Clint a quick smile.

Clint backed his horse out from between the other horses and reined away. He'd ridden only a few paces when, at the roar of a gunshot, he instinctively dropped low to the saddle. He spun the palomino to face the threat.

The Frenchman lay sprawled on his face in the dust, his arms and legs unmoving and splayed abnormally, a red splotch growing on his back. Vester Grumbles stood on the boardwalk, the smoking cap-and-ball in his hand. Gideon stared at his fallen master. Then Grumbles swung the muzzle to the slave.

Clint jerked the leather thong binding his sixty-foot woven rawhide reata to the saddle. Almost as quickly as he could form a loop, it cut the air. The reata dropped over a surprised Grumbles and snapped tight, throwing off his pistol's aim, then sending the Root's spinning away. Clint dallied the reata on the high pommel, spurred the palomino, and reined him away in the same motion.

With three of the big horse's powerful strides, Grumbles flew off the boardwalk and landed with a rolling dust-raising crash on the street near LaMont. When Clint was sure the Root's was left behind in the dirt, he reined the palomino and spun the animal to face the spitting man whose face had plowed a furrow in the dust.

"Don't even think about picking that Root's up," Clint warned, resting his hand on the butt of the Colt's pistol at his waist. Grumbles fought to get to his knees, then slowly climbed to his feet. He eyed the Root's, a few feet away.

"Don't," Clint repeated coldly.

Grumbles slowly worked the loop off his torso and discarded it, then cut his eyes back to the black man. His free hand came up to rub the side of his swollen face. "I don't care if you're white, green, or purple, free or slave, don't you ever raise your hands to me again

31

or you're a dead man."

Gideon, showing no emotion except for the tightly balled fists at his sides, nodded at Grumbles, who walked to his bay horse and mounted. He spun his horse away from where Clint sat, but paused long enough to look back over his shoulder. "We'll meet again," he called out.

"If we do, it could be the last time for you," Clint said, recoiling the reata, his tone in deadly earnest.

Grumbles gave his heels to the bay and galloped off, threading through the busy street. The saloon began to empty as men crowded out to view the fallen Frenchman.

Gideon stopped near the Root's, gave Clint a quizzical look, then, when Clint nodded, bent down and picked up the little pistol. He hurried to where Clint sat the palomino.

Barrel in hand, he offered the pistol to Clint, who shook his head. Gideon shoved the Root's in his belt and watched Clint in silence for a moment. He cleared his throat. "Sir, after I bury M'sieur LaMont, are you in need of a manservant?"

Clint was taken aback by the change in the man's speech, which even had the hint of a French accent. "You . . . you talk different now."

"I've lived and worked all my life among

the educated and studied their ways, but they preferred I speak in a manner they would not consider 'uppity.' " He glanced back at his fallen owner. "But there's no need for that now." He found Clint's eyes. "Might you be in need of a manservant?"

Clint chuckled at the thought. "You're a free man now. You don't need anyone. This is California, and she'll be coming into the Union free. You'll get along here fine. You got a punch like a mule." Clint watched the man's worried expression change to a blank one. Then Gideon's face lit. "Looks to me," Clint continued, offering encouragement, "like when you bury that Frenchman, you bury his chains along with him."

"A free man?" Gideon said, looking doubtful, then grinning. "A freedman!" But his grin faded. "I'll bury him, surely, for his mother and grandmother were kind to me and mine, and he and his brothers were kind enough in their arrogant way, but I need the manumission papers to be free."

"Not here. Like I said, California is gonna come in as a free state or she'll revolt and become an independent sovereign nation. Folks here, at least most of them, don't abide with owning slaves, nor with the kind of thinking your mas — your former owner had. Take care of yourself. I'm Clint Ryan," Clint said, and extended his hand. Gideon looked at him for a second, then grinned and shook.

"Gideon."

"No last name?" Clint asked, knowing from his experience with black sailors that many carried only one handle. "Hell, take his. He won't be needin' it."

Gideon muttered the name to himself a couple of times.

Clint tipped his wide-brimmed hat. "Nice to make your acquaintance, Gideon LaMont. It has a nice ring to it."

He spun the palomino and urged him away. "Good day, Mr. LaMont."

But the black didn't answer. He grinned, and repeated, shaking his head in wonderment, "Gideon LaMont, a freedman."

"Hold up there," a voice commanded from behind. Clint wheeled the horse, his hand finding the butt of the Colt's. A tall redheaded man stood with fire in his eyes, one chiseled granite hand clasping Gideon's shoulder roughly. In his other knotted hand he held a shortened 1841 Hall's rifle with a big .54-caliber bore — aimed at Clint's midsection.

"Keep your hands where I can see them and dismount. This Hall's carries a double charge and half a barrel fulla chopped-up square nails."

"And you'll cut down half the people on

this street if you let loose," Clint cautioned, his voice steady.

The man freed Gideon's shoulder and tapped the star on his chest. "If I do, it'll be legal."

Clint nudged the stallion back next to LaMont's body and dismounted, careful to keep his hands in plain sight of the man. Diablo snorted and pranced, nervous with the nearby dead man and smell of blood.

"I'm City Marshal's Deputy Thad McPherson. What the hell happened here?"

"Wasn't them," one of the miners called out from the crowded boardwalk. The others chimed in agreement.

McPherson glanced at them, then quickly returned his eyes to Clint. "Then who did the shootin'?"

Luther Baggs shouldered his way through the crowd. "A fella named Vester Grumbles."

"Shot him down in a fair fight?" McPherson asked, still watching Clint.

"Maybe . . . maybe not," Luther said with a shrug of his shoulders.

"Cold blood, from behind," Gideon offered.

"You keep your mouth shut." McPherson raised his voice derisively and glared at Gideon. "Your testimony's no better than that mule's." He motioned to a big Roman-nosed animal tied nearby.

Gideon folded his hands behind his back and shut up.

"He's right," Clint said. "The man was shot from behind. He never had a chance."

"I know Vester Grumbles," McPherson snapped. "He's no backshooter."

"Maybe not before today." Clint's voice remained steady. "Now he is."

"What's your name?" McPherson stepped forward, the muzzle of the Hall's held ready, his green eyes studying Clint carefully.

Clint glanced over the crowd before he answered. The last thing he wanted was for the law to discover the outstanding warrant for his arrest, and a name could put McPherson on that track. "I'm known as Lazo."

"That some kind of greaser name?" McPherson asked, his mouth pulling back in a lazy smirk.

"It's a Mexican name," Clint stated coldly.

"What's your other name?" McPherson's thumb never moved from the big hammer of the Hall's.

"Lazo. That's all there is."

"Well, Lazo, you be on your way." The deputy motioned with his stubby gun.

Clint wasted no time and mounted. He hesitated before he spurred Diablo, then looked back at the deputy. "Mr. LaMont there is a free man and he had nothing to do with this.

Ask any man who was in the saloon."

Half the crowd on the boardwalk chimed in their agreement. The rest sullenly held their tongues. Surprised, Gideon shook his head, fully expecting a lynch mob to emerge from the crowd like the head of Cleopatra's deadly asp from a basket of figs.

"You got a name?" McPherson asked Gideon.

"Gideon . . . Gideon LaMont."

"What's this man's handle?" McPherson poked the still body at Gideon's feet.

"He's Henri . . . Masters," Gideon said, his voice gaining confidence, but he glanced at Clint to judge his reaction.

Clint smiled, but only with his eyes. The former slave was learning fast.

"Did you know him?" McPherson was beginning to doubt the whole exchange.

"He was my associate. A fine man," Gideon said, smiling a little too broadly. "Bought a lot of enslaved folks and set them free. I owe him a lot and I'll see to his buryin'."

"Good," McPherson said, but his expression still reflected doubt. "That'll save the city a little money."

"I got a row to plow," Clint said, and spun the stallion away.

"Don't plow it too far," McPherson snapped. "I may want to talk with you again."

37

"I'll be around," Clint's voice rang out, but he didn't turn, and Diablo plodded unhurriedly down the road.

"Get this man off the street," McPherson instructed, and Clint heard Gideon's voice, strong and clear.

"Yes, sir."

Then the big horse wound its way into the crowded street out of earshot. Clint reined away, out of sight of the trouble, at the first intersection.

As the stallion clomped along, kicking dust in front of him, Clint decided he had had enough of the city. He yearned for the clean fresh-smelling countryside. He spurred the palomino into a canter and headed for the sand hills that ringed three sides of the growing town.

Just as he neared the last of the tents, two vaqueros flanked him, riding at the same pace.

The man on his right, astride a big red roan, doffed his sombrero. "You are the man they call El Lazo?"

"I've been called that, by friends in the south."

"You must come with us."

Clint rested his hand on the butt of the Colt's pistol shoved in his belt. "And who the hell are you?"

"I am Sancho Guiterrez, the head vaquero

and *segundo* of Rancho del Rio Ancho." The man snatched a leather pouch from his belt and handed it across to Clint. It weighed heavy with gold — and gold was something Clint would need if he was to stock the Kaweah ranch.

"And where do we ride?" Clint asked in a considerably more agreeable tone.

"We don't ride. We take the boat. To Rancho del Rio Ancho, on the river Sacramento, the home of Don Carlos Vega."

Again Clint hefted the weighty pouch. "Lead the way, amigo." He smiled, tucked the pouch into his belt, and followed the vaqueros, who reined around and galloped for the bay.

CHAPTER THREE

The anchor lantern cast a pale circle and reflected off the encroaching fog, a single glowing eye glowering from the mizzenmast of the full-rigged packet ship *Amnity*.

At one hundred seventy-five feet, the *Amnity* reigned among the largest of the more than eight hundred hulls anchored in the San Francisco Bay. The dark and fog precluded admiration of her black-painted hull, green-painted deckhouses, and bright varnished bends, as the four hull planks below the deckline were called. Her decks were naked pine, continually holystoned with sand to keep them free of stain. Her mainmast rose one hundred sixty feet from the water to her main truck; her foremast was only slightly shorter; and her mizzenmast, near where her captain stood on the quarterdeck watching with interest, was only slightly shorter yet.

Fully loaded, the packet's main deck lay nine feet above the water. Now, her holds empty, she rode at fourteen. The quarterdeck rose another six.

With no idea what was happening, the fourteen feet seemed a thousand to Apolonia Vega as she spun upward, suspended from a light block and tackle, still bound in her sackcloth and trussed like a keg of molasses. She expelled the breath she had been holding only when she felt the reassuring support of the solid deck. The sounds of the quiet creaking of the rigging and yardarms were unfamiliar to her, but the slight roll told her she was aboard ship.

On the quarterdeck in the darkness, Isaac Banyon stood with his large sun-reddened hands clasped behind his back, his booted feet spread wide in a stance acquired from twenty-five years riding the pitching decks of a dozen ships. He wore no mustache, but his steel gray side beard joined chin whiskers in the New England manner, and the whiskers fell in waves to the middle of his wide chest. He was often misjudged as fat, for he was as deep as he was broad, and his girth at the waist far exceeded even his barrel chest. But he carried little extra weight; rather, he was built much like the hogshead barrels the *Amnity* normally carried in her hold. Many men would have allowed themselves to go to fat as master and owner of the *Amnity*. But not Cap'n Moses, as his men referred to him in private, for his piercing gray eyes and wavy beard portrayed that biblical image. Among other attributes he carried from his Quaker upbringing was a reverence for hard work. And he neither drank the demon rum nor smoked tobacco.

He served the Lord through his own liberal interpretation of the Bible, and he served himself — mostly himself — with hard work, and expected no less from his men. His was one of the few ships that had not lost a man to the diggin's, for he ruled her with an iron hand — and it rested on the butt of an Aston cap-and-ball pistol that always protruded from his belt while in port.

Bringing one of his rawboned, bony-knuckled hands up to his chin, he rubbed his whiskers, watching the men hoist their fragile burden aboard. They got her to her feet and guided her, still bound, gagged, and blindfolded, aft to the communal passenger quarters, disappearing into the hatchway below the quarterdeck.

Banyon clasped his hands behind his back and paced the windward side of the quarterdeck, satisfied that this would be a profitable voyage. Profitable indeed, as his cargo continued to grow in quantity and, with the addition of Apolonia Vega, certainly in quality.

" 'Tis the devil's work ye do, Isaac Banyon."
His wife, Lucretia, startled him from behind.

"Damn ye, woman," he snapped, "ye move around this ship like Satan's own apparition. It is the Lord's work I do, as I have always done."

"Don't blaspheme in my presence." She drew the dark cloak she wore tighter around her face while Isaac glared at her. After more than a year on board she still had the sallow withered look of a winter-trapped, parlor-bound New Englander. "Trading in flesh is not the Lord's —"

"Quiet yourself!" He took a step forward and she gave a step, her watery eyes wide. "The Good Book supports my every act. 'Smite the Philistines,' it says. The heathen China Marys and the papist whores of California who follow the edicts of a Roman master have no place in God's perfect world. They are the Philistines of our time."

Turning with a whirl of her cape, Lucretia faded back out of sight. Banyon heard her footfalls on the ladder to the main deck. Then her voice rang out clearly: "Do ye unto others, Isaac Banyon."

"Get back to your tatting, woman, or ye'll find yourself on the next ship back to Pennsylvania."

"Ye'd like that, left alone with the devil's

cargo." Her voice disappeared with her footfalls.

He should never have allowed her to come
along. *A fool's errand*, he cursed himself. Had
he any idea he would be involved in trading
the goods he now carried, he would have left
her home. But how was he to guess? Opportunity came in strange ways, and a man had
to be ready.

Banyon clasped his hands behind his back
and paced the rail with angry strides. The deck
rang with his heavy footfalls; then his anger
wore off and his steps quieted. After a few
moments he·stopped, dug into the pocket of
his heavy woolen coat, and pulled out a pipe.
He knocked out the dottle and repacked it,
content with his place in the scheme of things.
He lit up with a sulfurhead that flared for a
moment in the darkness.

Before Banyon had half finished the pipe,
Harlan Stoddard, his first mate, scrambled up
the quarterdeck ladder.

"No problems with this one." Stoddard
smiled, revealing yellowed teeth beneath the
soup-strainer. He rubbed the back of his thick
neck with a ham-sized hand. " 'Twas clean
as a newly honed knife blade."

"And is she the beauty it was said she is?"

"Even better, I would say, Cap'n. The best
of the lot."

"Good. Set an extra deck watch tonight, just in case ye were followed."

"No chance of that, but as ye wish." Harlan Stoddard flashed a grin that reflected his yellowed teeth in the lantern light, then turned to head for the fo'c'sle and to call the watch. His massive shoulders gathered and he put both hands on the rails. With the skill of a man long at sea, he slid to the lower deck without putting a foot on a rung.

"Did ye have ol' Abner take her a smock?" Banyon called after him.

"Aye, Cap'n, like always."

Banyon waited until his first mate disappeared into the forward fo'c'sle hatchway, then started aft. His pace quickened and he took the half ladder two rungs at a time. He entered his wide cabin and was disappointed to see Lucretia not in bed but sitting in her rocker. Even in the cabin and already in her heavy nightgown, she wore a flowered coal-scuttle bonnet. She read the Bible.

Lucretia looked up, her eyes still reflecting condemnation, but her voice had softened. "Are you ready to retire?" she asked.

"Not quite yet. You go ahead. I want to check the rudder gear . . . been binding up a bit." He moved to the supply closet, picking a swinging coal-oil lantern off its hook as he passed. Entering, he pulled the door shut behind him and carefully turned the lantern down until it barely glowed. Then he knelt and pulled away the deck boards where the control cables passed below through the closet to the rudder block and tackle ten feet below. Carefully, quietly, he climbed down into the dank musty passageway with barely enough room for his massive bulk, until he reached the lower deck level. Moving forward a few feet into a cleft, he searched the splintery bulkhead in the darkness and found the tin can top that he had carefully placed over a quarter-inch borehole. He swung it aside and peered through.

"I shall *not* remove my gown," the girl's voice nervously rang through the plank walls.

By all that's holy, she is a beauty, Banyon thought as he pressed closer to the peephole to watch the slender girl, whose gleaming black tresses hung to her two-hand-span waist. Dark eyes flashed, contrasting with a perfect complexion as light and clear as alabaster.

"Either you'll do it, or the cap'n will have the men do it for you," cackled old Abner, the ship's supercargo, his voice whistling through the spaces of missing teeth. Then, gaining a touch of compassion, his look softened and he ran a bony hand through his wispy hair. He scratched his liver-spotted pate. "Please, lass, take off your clothes and put the smock on. 'Tis a decent if simple gown and 'tis an order from the cap'n. Put your'n in the sack and I'll store it for ya."

"But why? Why am I here?"

"There are others like ya in the passenger's cabin. You'll be able to join your own kind as soon as you're settled in a bit. I'll give ya ten minutes, lass. Then, if you've not complied, I'll have to tell the cap'n, and he'll send the men."

She glared in anger and weighed the alternatives. "Then leave me."

As old Abner pulled the door to the little cabin shut, Banyon pressed so close that he could feel the wood grain in his cheek. The girl turned her back to the door and faced the peephole, then began to unbutton the tightly fitted jacket and blouse. Banyon's breath quickened when she slipped out of the jacket and her full breasts were outlined under the white chemise she wore beneath, dark-peaked circles testifying to the chill of the cabin. She untied her long skirt and it fell away to the deck. Her legs were slender and long, and smooth below the white pantalettes that covered them to just above the knee, exposing the skin between them and her calf-length stockings.

"Damn," he mumbled when she picked up the smock and slipped it on over her head without removing her undergarments. She stopped and stared at the wall, and Isaac held his breath. After a second she bent and recovered the skirt, stuffing it and the jacket into the sack she had been provided.

A sharp knock on the door snapped her head around. "Enter," she said, her voice as cold as the bay that lapped the hull just outside the cabin.

"Are ya done?" Abner asked, standing in the hatchway.

Without speaking, she handed him the sack. He ruffled through it, then looked up.

"Sorry, lass," he said, "but you'll have to shed the boots an' . . ." his eyes found the floor, "an' whatever else ye have on under."

"What?"

"All but the smock."

"*Chingaso*," she spat.

"Don't understand that Mexican." He smiled wanly, showing gaps where teeth should be. "An' it's probably jus' as well."

"Out," she said, and shoved the door in his face.

Banyon felt the grain of the wood as his eye bulged, but she merely raised the hem of the gown and worked the ties at the back of her chemise.

"Isaac, are you all right down there?" Lucretia's voice rang out, and Isaac jerked back, cracking his head on a crossbeam.

He hurried out of the cleft and glowered up into her pale face, lit by the lantern she held.

"I'll be along. Get ye to bed, woman."

"Is the steering gear all right?" she asked, but her voice rang with sarcasm. " 'Tis the fifth time you've checked it since we've been in San Francisco Bay."

"To bed, woman. I'm coming up."

She was in bed, asleep, or pretending to be, with her bony flannel-gowned back to him, by the time he had stripped to his faded red long johns and joined her.

Though neither of them could hear the quiet sobs from the cabin below, Isaac Banyon forgot his prayers, his thoughts centered on more earthly matters, and it was a long time before his breathing evened out to match Lucretia's.

CHAPTER
FOUR

It was as dark as a blind man's holiday by the time Clint and the vaqueros neared the shore where Rancho del Rio Ancho stretched for over four miles. By that time Clint, Sancho, and Enrico Alverez were fast friends.

The two vaqueros were men not unlike those Clint had spent the last three years with during his meanderings through southern California. Like most vaqueros, at first Sancho and Enrico had been skeptical of a tall, sandy-haired, blue-eyed Anglo who wore the embroidered jacket and *calzonevas* of the vaquero, but after several hours aboard the little donkey-engine steam-powered scow and conversations about mutual acquaintances they had all ridden with, he was accepted.

As gruff as he had seemed at first, Sancho turned out to be a comical man quick to smile and full of stories. Even more importantly, he was a second cousin to Inocente Ruiz, the *segundo,* or foreman, of Rancho del Robles Viejos in Santa Barbara, where Clint had worked for a while. It was Inocente who Clint had saved from a sure death with his quick and proficient reata work — and who had given Clint his Californio nickname, El Lazo, the lasso.

The scow rounded a bend and Sancho rose from his seat on a pile of cast iron bound for the diggin's. Stretching, he kicked Enrico, who was dozing on the deck.

"It is time, Lazo," Sancho said as Enrico climbed to his feet. They picked their way through barrels and crates to where their three stallions were tethered. The men saddled and bridled the horses, then waved to the captain of the little work boat, who steered as close to the shore as he could in the darkness. They mounted and Clint leaned forward in the saddle, squinting into the black void, searching for the wharf or landing he was sure would mark their departure spot.

Instead, Sancho's exuberant yell startled him as the vaquero gave spurs to his stallion. The big bay lunged forward, gathered its powerful haunches under it, and cleared the scow's low rail. Enrico followed, and Clint gave his spurs to Diablo. The big horse hesitated a half second, then followed. They hit the water with a tremendous splash and disappeared into the murky depths. Clint kicked free of the stirrups and slipped out of the saddle, clinging to the horn and allowing the animal freedom to swim. As he had learned to do so many times in the last three years, he depended on the big horse to get him out of trouble.

The stallion stretched its neck forward and with powerful strokes of its long legs soon found the muddy bottom. Clint walked out behind, with a death grip on the reins. The palomino shook like a dog while Clint wiped water from his own hair and eyes.

"Eye, yi, yi!" Sancho yelled from nearby. "The Sacramento, she is cold for summer-time."

Clint mounted and waited for Sancho and Enrico, who looked like drowned kittens with their dark hair matted to their bean-brown faces as they rode up beside him.

"We ride, Lazo, to hot coffee and tortillas," Sancho said. Without awaiting an answer, he spurred his horse into the darkness. Clint followed at a lope, barely able to see the trail in the moonlight. They rode for an hour before Sancho drew rein, setting the bay back on its haunches.

In the distance a light glowed.

"It is the hacienda, amigo," he said to Clint. "It is only a few more minutes."

As they neared they passed through a vineyard, and Clint could make out the whitewashed walls of a big adobe in the moonglow. Through a tall arched gate in the wall, they came into a courtyard. A boy hurried to take their horses, and Clint reluctantly handed his over. It had been a hard ride and he was concerned about the palomino.

Sancho sensed his reluctance. "He will be well cared for, Lazo."

Their roweled spurs rang as they made their way to the big carved door, which swung aside before they reached it. Wall sconces holding a dozen candles each lit the entry, and the tall well-dressed don extended his hand to Clint.

"El Lazo," he said as Clint shook. "I am Don Carlos Vega. Welcome to Rancho del Rio Ancho."

The distinguished man led Clint into a huge dim living room with a wide fireplace at one end. Another man sat in one of four chairs, his legs splayed in front of him, a crystal snifter cradled in one hand.

As they approached, Don Carlos made the introduction. "Lazo, this is my daughter's betrothed, Don Gaspar Cota."

The man rose and extended his hand, but his look was doubtful and hard. He sported a thin mustache, lost in his wide round face.

Clint attempted a smile, but was unsuccessful. The man's grip was like shaking one of the salted cod that had been barreled on board the scow they had just left — dry and lifeless.

"I must be frank, Señor Lazo," Gaspar Cota said as he collapsed back into the chair. "You are invited here over my objection. This is a matter best handled by the Vegas and the Cotas."

"What matter?" Clint asked.

"Please be seated." Don Vega motioned him to a chair. "Sancho, please bring another snifter for Señor Lazo . . . and pour one for Enrico and yourself before you leave."

Clint found a seat in one of the high-backed leather chairs, nodded his thanks to Sancho for the brandy, and waited.

Don Vega leaned against the fireplace, staring into its low flames. It crackled and spat a few sparks out onto the smooth well-packed earthen floor. The don ignored them. The small fire was the only light in the room other than a pair of candlesticks on a table lining the wall. The don remained silent until he heard the door close, signaling his vaqueros' retreat.

"How is the brandy?" he asked, but didn't wait for an answer. "We make it right here on the rancho. I have heard a great deal about you, Señor Lazo. I feel fortunate that you were

54

seen near Monterey on your way to San Francisco. We had a most unfortunate occurrence only yesterday. My daughter, Gaspar's betrothed, was abducted."

"By whom?" Clint asked.

"We know very little. She was riding, as she did every day. She was miles from the hacienda near the river, being watched, as is our custom, by her *dueña* and her driver in a buggy."

"And?"

"She was dragged from her horse by four Chinese. José, the driver, attempted to go to her rescue, but he was shot. He died only a few hours ago. But he was able to tell us that it was Chinese who did this thing."

"I am surprised, Don Vega. I have known many Chinese, sailed with them on a number of vessels. I even speak a little of their language. They respect and fear the law . . . more than most."

"These obviously did not," Gaspar said coldly. "Had you Anglos not brought those heathens to our shores —"

Don Vega interrupted him. "You are an Anglo, Lazo, but have the reputation of being a friend to those of us who once ruled California." Don Vega took a sip of his brandy, studying Clint's reaction.

"Like most men, I have many friends and

a few enemies, Don Vega. If I can be of service to you, I would be pleased."

"The Ortiz and the Padilla families have daughters missing also. And the wife of Don Robles has disappeared. At first I thought these girls merely ran away, probably with Anglos whose pockets were packed with gold. I would have understood why Don Robles's wife might have fled him. But now . . . now I think there is some plot at hand. All of them live near San Francisco on San Pablo Bay, so the water seems to be a common thread . . . if there is one." He again looked into the fire, the reflection of the flames dancing in his eyes. "I would go myself, but English is now the language of preference there; I speak little of it and, of course, no Chinese. And San Francisco is a quandary to me, Señor." For the first time the old don began to show his frustration.

"Things are not the same as they were before you Anglos came. Killings, robberies . . . and now kidnappings." He raised his eyes from the fire, and Clint realized Don Carlos was pleading. It was not a thing the proud man seemed accustomed to. "Would you please find my daughter, and return her to me?"

"Have you contacted the law?" Clint asked.

"Ha!" Gaspar said, tossing the last of his

drink down his throat.

"The law, Señor," the old don said with derision, "is only for the Anglo. The Californio is only laughed at and ridiculed and treated like an interloper in his own land if he appeals to the law. You may talk to the law if you wish. Maybe they will listen to an Anglo. For us, it is fruitless."

Clint quietly digested that. He had seen the attitude of many Anglos, particularly those who had arrived as a result of the gold rush. Just as Don Carlos said, they treated the Mexicans as if they were the foreigners. Hell, Mexican miners even had to pay a thirty-dollar-a-year mining tax — a foreigner's tax — to mine land they had occupied for two hundred years. It was easy to understand Don Vega's distrust and disrespect for the Anglo law.

"I will do what I can," Clint offered reluctantly. What he really wanted to find out was how to go about getting title to the Kaweah ranch. But the land would be there when he found the time.

"And I will ride with you," Gaspar said. Standing, he tucked his chin back and puffed up like a ruffled grouse strutting before a hen.

Clint eyed the rather pudgy, round-faced Californio don with the finely trimmed narrow mustache, and did not picture him as a great deal of help in any endeavor. More importantly, he sensed that this would be work for one man working alone. The less dust raised, the better.

Ignoring the man's offer, which had more the inflection of a command, Clint turned his attention back to Don Vega. "Why are you convinced they are in San Francisco?"

"Their tracks led downriver, at least for a few hundred yards, where they boarded a small boat." Frustration rang in his voice. "I know it is very little, Lazo. But it is all the information we have. I will pay you well if you succeed. There is little gold, but I have some of the finest horseflesh in California. Purebred Andalusians."

Clint's ears perked up. "Just how many horses would you consider fair, if I returned your daughter safely?"

The old don hesitated a minute before he answered. "Forty head?"

"Forty head of my choice?" Clint asked.

"Any among the four hundred or so on the ranch, with the exception of our personal riding stock."

Clint extended his hand and shook with the old man.

"Then we ride!" Gaspar said. "First thing in the morning."

"I'll be going alone," Clint said, his gaze

finding the small dark eyes of Gaspar Cota.

"No!" Gaspar slammed a fist on the arm of the chair. "This is my fiancée, and I and my vaqueros will ride with you. There were many Chinese, and one man —"

"Don Vega," Clint said, ignoring Gaspar. "I ride alone. As you said, this is a job for an Anglo."

"Carlos," Gaspar sputtered, his jowls shaking, "I told you it was unnecessary for you to call this . . . this Anglo."

Clint gave his back to Gaspar, facing the old don. "I will leave now, Don Vega, if you would be so kind as to have some tortillas and meat packed, and to describe your daughter to me while I saddle up."

"Momentito," Don Vega said, and walked to the table holding the two candles. With reverence he picked up a small framed object from between the candles, walked back, and handed it to Clint.

"She is beautiful," Clint said respectfully, studying the tiny daguerreotype. "May I keep this?"

"Of course. . . ." Don Vega's voice wavered. "But I want it back, no matter what."

Clint nodded, then started for the door, with Don Vega close behind.

"If you will not accompany me, I will search without you," Gaspar yelled from behind.

Don Vega stopped; his shoulders straightened as he turned back. "Don Cota, Apolonia was my daughter long before she became your betrothed, and she is your betrothed only at my bequest. You may search the hills of Rancho del Rio Ancho or the Cota rancho or even Sacramento City all you wish." His voice hardened. "But stay away from San Francisco and allow Señor Lazo to do what I am paying him to do. Mexican Californios are not among San Francisco's most admired citizens at the moment. You will do more harm than good there and possibly get yourself killed." He glared at Gaspar. "And I would find that difficult to explain to your father."

Gaspar Cota sputtered, but was unable to say anything more. Don Vega yelled some instructions down a hallway, then slammed the big carved door and followed Clint across the wide courtyard to the barn. While they walked, the don described Apolonia Vega's size, voice, and manner.

Clint led the palomino, now grained and watered, outside, and was met by an Indian woman with a muslin sack full of food.

He thanked her and tied it on the back of the saddle.

The don laid a slender hand on Clint's shoulder. "I am sorry there is no more gold to pay you, El Lazo —"

"I would help even if there were no horses, Don Vega."

"Horses we have. The finest in California. I will give them willingly."

"Five stallions, thirty-five mares," Clint said, mounting.

"Willingly," the old man said. "You must want to become a breeder. You can do no better than Rancho del Rio Ancho stock." He paused, and Clint caught the glimmer of wetness in his old eyes in the dim moonlight. "I would give all to have my Apolonia back. Her mother is gone, and she is the last of the Vegas."

"Even though boats leave no tracks, I will find her, Don Vega."

"Vaya con Dios." The old man raised his arm and waved as Clint loped his palomino out of the courtyard and then gave the animal its head. The horse would have to find the trail back to the river, which Clint knew it would do with no problem. Then it was up to Clint.

He hoped his task would prove only a hundred times as difficult.

He feared it might be a million or more.

CHAPTER FIVE

Clint had to ride along the river all the way to Benicia before he was able to catch a morning boat and return to San Francisco. Benicia, with its wide back bay and tidal estuary, reminded him of Mystic, Connecticut, where as a young boy he had been indentured to a tanner.

During the long voyage from Ireland, Clint's parents and sister had died from the dreaded cholera — when he was but seven years old. His time in Mystic, as an indentured servant, had not been pleasant, but he had learned a trade and how to work — and when he ran away to sea it had been easier for him than it might have been for a wet-behind-the-ears country boy.

The sun was straight overhead by the time the scow pulled alongside the old iron revenue steamer *James K. Polk*, now high and dry and used as a wharf. An irate landing agent started to berate Clint when he led the palomino onto the gangplank and crossed the deck of the *Polk*. A sharp look at the man quelled his ardor, and Clint reached the hundred-yard-long pier that had been constructed from the landward rail of the *Polk* across the tide-out mud flats.

When Clint and his palomino clomped off the pier onto the sand, he mounted, rode a few steps to another beached ship, the *Apollo*, and tied his horse to a rail outside. The *Apollo* lay buried six feet deep in the sand. Six-by-six-inch posts at forty-five-degree angles buttressed her hull and gave the impression of a ship under construction on the ways. But she would never feel the sea under her bow again. Her hold now housed a plank bar and tables — and over fifty drinking and gambling men. Her inner bulkheads had been torn away to open her up. Ports covered with waxed paper to let in the light but keep out the kelp flies were cut into her hull well below what would have been the waterline.

Clint figured this was as good a place as any to begin his quest. At least a few hours listening to the scuttlebutt on the waterfront was the best way to start.

He sipped a beer, ate a couple of pickled eggs for lunch, and moved from table to table, where he found nothing but newly arrived men awaiting transportation up the river to the gold fields. One thing he did discover was that the day before, over a thousand Chinese had arrived aboard five different ships. Maybe circulating among the city's permanent residents would turn up something more.

As Clint started up Montgomery Street, he passed two other wooden ships, each rapidly becoming a skeleton of ribs as workmen stripped away their rigging, planking, line, and canvas for use in constructing more permanent structures — permanent at least until the next fire swept through the town. He had overheard an ex-captain at the *Apollo* brag that he had gotten more for his ship as building supplies in San Francisco than he could have sold her for as a working vessel in New York.

Before Clint had made his way for one block through the workmen and drays and crowds of miners, the sand street gave way to boards, and Diablo's hooves clattered hollowly. The tents and clapboards gave way to wood-frame and even a few brick-and-metal-shuttered buildings. He glanced at one of the only canvas-covered businesses on this block and decided to stop. If anyone in San Francisco, or any other town, knew what was going on, it would be a barber.

PHILAS PHISTER'S TONSORIAL PALACE AND

BATH EMPORIUM, as foot-high red letters on a canvas banner proclaimed, was hardly as big as its name. A canvas roof stretched across a twenty-foot lot between two permanent two-story buildings. Half the frontage was occupied by two tall stools and a brick fire pit. The pit, billowing black smoke and obviously constructed from scraps and broken bricks left over from the construction of its neighbors, roared with flame. The other half of the frontage was enclosed by a ten-by-ten-foot tent ensuring the relative privacy of two leather tubs.

A one-eyed Chinaman, not more than four feet tall, with a braided queue protruding from under a skullcap and dangling to below his rump, carried buckets from a copper boiler on the fire pit into the bathing tent, where curses and yowls were emitted each time he filled the occupied tubs with boiling water.

Two barbers, each perfectly coifed and sporting upturned mustaches that would shame a Turk, worked away at the stools, clipping and combing a line of men that stretched across the boardwalk and into the board street.

Around each stool lay a foot-deep semicircle of variegated hair.

Clint didn't want to waste time in line, but the surest way to pushing up daisies was to crowd in front of mud-soaked placer miners eyeing a hot bath — unless, of course, it was crowding into the line across the street under the golden-lettered sign which read, MADAM DUPRE'S FRENCH SUPPER HOUSE AND ENTERTAINMENT EMPORIUM.

It seemed Montgomery Street had an undeclared battle under way for the longest-named emporium and gaudiest sign. This one, Clint had heard, was the finest brothel on the newly christened Barbary Coast, and the only one that bragged a white woman, though she had never been seen outside the front door. The only way it could be proven was by paying up. The establishment's name was only slightly longer than Phister's, but its line was four times as long — even though the rumor was that the shortest time a man could spend upstairs at Madam Dupre's cost five ounces of gold.

Clint tied Diablo to a hitching rail and stepped to the end of the barber's line. His own sandy locks hung to his shoulders; the sight of his ears was a memory. The barber would provide more than much-needed information. Clint waited, and visited with the men in line as he did so, but learned nothing of value.

It took him an hour to reach the stool.

"How long is it gonna be afore you get back to see us?" the barber asked as he stropped the razor he had used to shave the last man.

"Trim 'er down and lay on the foo-foo so I can find my ears and turn a few ladies' heads," Clint said, returning the barber's smile.

"That's a laugh, friend. Hell, I ain't seen a woman, at least not a white one, since I left Philadelphia almost a year ago."

The man introduced himself and draped Clint in a soggy, spotted cloth. Clint was pleased to learn that he had landed in the chair of Philas Phister himself. While Philas lathered him up for the shave, Clint managed to pose one two-part question.

"Just what is the lady situation hereabouts, and what the hell do all these Chinese do for women?"

As barbers are so adept at doing, Philas talked the whole time he shaved and trimmed Clint. Three of the man's nonstop sentences stayed with Clint, whose ears were now plainly visible.

"The newest feature in town, the Barracoon, is the only place for a man to find a woman, at least for a keeper, if he can't find an Indian girl to entice away from her brave with a poke full of gold, and you can't find one there at the Barracoon least for a few days," was the first.

"There are no white women who show their faces on the streets, except for Sultana Mulvany, and I've yet to have the pleasure of seeing her," was the second.

"Tok Wu 'Huly Up' Hong is the man to ask if you want to know anything, and I mean anything, about the Chinese, 'cause he is one of the few John Chinamen who speaks any English a-tall," was the third.

Clint gladly paid the two dollars and fifty cents for what would have cost two bits in ordinary times. The information was well worth it.

Smelling so good he could hardly stand himself, he left Philas and set out to find Huly Up Hong. Even Diablo turned his head and eyed Clint, as if wondering if he had been loaded with a bushel of lilacs.

Telegraph Hill rose over the bay between the foot of Montgomery Street, where the majority of the waterfront activity took place, and the distant narrow opening to the Pacific, christened the Golden Gate by John Fremont. The early settlers of Yerba Buena and, later, San Francisco, had scrambled up the hill to watch ships entering the harbor — but that was a thing of the past. The west side of Telegraph sported hundreds of Chinese shacks and the east side half as many Italian shanties — with a no-man's land in between. It was rapidly becoming the worst section of San Francisco, other than Clark's Point, where the waterfront degenerated into the worst nest of shanghaiers, thieves, and murderers on the Barbary Coast. None of the thirty San Francisco city marshal's deputies would venture into the area without a number of their mates watching their backs.

Clint left the board-covered streets and followed a winding road, Calle de Fundación. Most of Chinatown teemed with shacks constructed from every imaginable scrap, but a few buildings were of lumber. Men in black cotton pants and long-sleeved coats or robes hurried about, each as if he had a mission. Few horses were in the streets, but small cages of ducks, chickens, pigeons, and an occasional pig or goat occupied every crack and cranny around the crowded tents and shacks.

Every available spot of earth not used for a dwelling or road or cage was growing something. The permanent buildings had window boxes at each opening, and each had a well-tended herb garden. An occasional flash of color marked a spot where hunger or flavor gave way to beauty, and a flower grew.

Paper lanterns hung from the front of every shanty. Chinatown, when the Chinese wanted it to be, was better lit than any other section of the city.

Clint had spent enough time aboard ships with Chinese crew members to know that crowded conditions did not daunt them. Where other sailors might have messy bunks and chests in which nothing could be found, the Chinese, always relegated to the smallest and most confined of the fo'c'sle bunks, were a picture of order and — if it could be said about a fo'c'sle — beauty. A Chinese could dump a bucket of cod, a cork float, and a piece of seaweed on the deck, and within seconds it would be arranged as a still life worthy of the walls of a cathedral. A Chinese bunk always held some decoration, if only a paper design along the bulkhead or a hanging decoration that swayed with the roll of the ship. The Chinamen had gained Clint's respect, and he had become fast friends with a number of them during his seafaring days.

Clint dismounted in front of a shack, made from a rusted-out boiler and several partially rotted hull planks, that served as an eating establishment, and found a seat at one of two tables in front of it. Two Chinese at the other table glanced at him nervously, finished their bowls of rice and their cups of tea, and hurried into the dirt street.

An old man stuck his head out of the rusted boiler section and eyed Clint with suspicion. Obviously he got few white customers. Clint reached to the other table, picked up a handleless teacup, and motioned to him. The man disappeared and quickly reappeared with a teapot and spotlessly clean cup, then filled it for Clint.

"Tok Wu Hong?" Clint asked the man, who shrugged his shoulders. Clint reached into his pocket and removed a tiny one-dollar gold piece and placed it on the table. "Tok Wu Hong," he repeated, pointing to the tiny gold piece, then to the old man.

A hint of a smile tugged at the corners of the old man's mouth and he disappeared into the boiler. Clint was startled as a small boy bolted past him, then disappeared down the street.

Before Clint had finished his third cup of tea, the boy returned, with a squat square-shouldered man following. The man, unremarkable in his plain black robes, bowed politely in front of Clint.

"I am Tok Wu Hong," he said, finding Clint's eyes for only a fraction of a second. His own black eyes continually worked the street, the small yard where the tables sat, the sky, and every other conceivable target.

"You're the man known as Huly Up Hong."

He bowed. "Your humble servant, honorable one."

Clint motioned him to sit, and he did. The old man refilled Clint's cup and poured one for Hong. Clint waited until the old man shuffled back inside the boiler. "I need information about some Chinese."

Hong's dark eyes quickly found Clint's, then cut away.

"And why do you seek these men? A man's life would be of no value if he gave information about his own that might lead to their injury."

"If these men were stopped, it would be for the good of all honorable Chinese. They have taken a girl. Maybe more than one. All of California will soon rise up against the Chinese if these men are not found and this girl returned."

Hong studied him. "It would be a terrible thing for the wrath of the white devils to fall upon the Celestials. There is only one man who can speak of this with you."

"And who might that be?"

"You are willing to go alone to see him?"

"I came alone to see you."

"Are you willing to pay Tok Wu ten dollars in gold?"

"I would pay one dollar."

"I thought you wished badly to see this man."

"I thought you believed it would be a terrible thing for the wrath of the white devils to fall upon the Celestials."

"I think it would be maybe five dollars worth of terrible."

"Fine. I wish to see this man five dollars worth."

Hong rose and stuck his head into the boiler shack. He spoke rapidly, then the boy ran out and around Clint and down the street again. Hong strode past Clint. "Have your five dollars in hand. Follow me, huly up, huly up, prease," Hong instructed, and was half a block down the road, living up to his nickname, before Clint was mounted and following.

Hong walked deeper into Chinatown, Clint following on Diablo. By the time they had covered three blocks, the boy approached and spoke to Hong, who looked up at Clint and extended the flat of his palm.

Clint dropped a five-dollar gold piece into Hong's hand. Hong bit it, testing its validity, then smiled briefly.

"Zhang Ho will see you. I am surprised." He hurried on, and Clint nudged the palomino after him.

One block of structures was better constructed than the others, and Hong stopped in front of the only two-story brick building Clint had noticed in all of Chinatown. It stood without adornment, with board shutters covering the windows.

Hong climbed the four steps to the stoop and rapped sharply on the plain-paneled door while Clint dismounted and tied Diablo to a single wrought-iron post with a ring in it. By the time Clint had loosened Diablo's cinch and started for the door, Hong was descending the stairs.

"I am not needed here," he said, and disappeared down the street.

The door creaked open and a boy of no more than ten, barefoot and dressed in ragged cotton pants and shirt, bowed when he saw Clint.

"Zhang Ho, please," Clint said, and the boy opened the door wider and stepped aside. Clint crossed the threshold and waited for his eyes to adjust to the darkness. He made out a man sitting in a corner on the floor. A frayed mat in front of him held a cup and a bowl half filled with a meager portion of rice and some scraps of meat, and a wooden cane topped by a carved dragon's head lay on the floor next to him. A wisp of pure white hair stuck out from a hooded cloak that covered his old head, in contrast to a pure black mustache that hung a foot down on either side of his tightly drawn mouth. His ragged cloak hung past his shoulders to the floor.

The boy quietly disappeared out the front door, pulling it shut behind him. The room reeked of cheap incense and the smoke of a single candle, which also rested on the floor of the barren room in one far corner.

"You seek Ho?" Though the old man managed to raise his head, he seemed almost too feeble to talk.

"Yes. I understand he will speak to me of a problem that threatens both your people and mine."

"A thousand pardons, sir, but problems of *bai* not business of Celestials. It better to remain so." Clint had to strain to hear the old man. He moved closer.

"*Wan ri shenti, laodaye,*" Clint began, wishing him ten thousand years of health and calling him by the respectful term *old grandfather*. Then he smiled. "*Kai wanxiao,*" "You make a joke," Clint said, insisting that the problems of the whites in California must be the problems of the Chinese. He spoke slowly, haltingly, remembering all that his shipboard friends had taught him.

The old man had looked up in surprise when Clint offered his first words in Chinese, then regained his composure. He, too, changed to Chinese, but also spoke deliberately and slowly. "You speak the honorable language of Han."

"I am an ignorant man, old grandfather. I speak the Celestials' language only a little, but I come on an important mission that the honorable Zhang Ho must hear of."

The old man studied him carefully, then picked up his cane and labored to his feet.

Clint moved forward, put his hand under the old man's arm to steady him, and helped him up.

An inner door separated the room from what lay beyond, and the stooped old man creaked his way toward it. He stopped before he reached for the knob. "You are friend to Chinese?"

"I am a friend to any man who's a friend to me."

The old man studied him, then appeared satisfied with the answer. He turned the knob, and light flooded the room. Clint waited until the old man shuffled through, then followed. He stared at the great room, at least six times as large as the entry. The incense that graced the room wafted to him like a fresh high-mountain meadow. Colorful paneled screens adorned the walls — scenes of ancient China, intricate paintings of gardens and birds. A carved mahogany screen stood nearby — a dozen Chinese warriors doing battle with a great fire-breathing dragon.

Clint shook his head in wonder, but was even more amazed when the old man straightened and shed the ragged cloak he wore. He ran his hand through his hair, putting the wisp of white back into place. He seemed to lose twenty years with the cloak and gain twenty pounds as his shoulders squared and his spine straightened. Another Chinese hurried forward and held a fine embroidered black and red silk robe for him. He donned it and extended his hand to Clint.

"I am Zhang Ho," he said from under a full head of black hair, the single streak of white tucked carefully into place. "What do you wish of the Fu Sang Tong?"

CHAPTER
SIX

Clint almost chuckled over the ruse, but didn't.

"Would you like to take tea while you tell me of this 'mutual problem'?" Ho asked politely as they moved across the room and reclined on silk pillows, separated by a low carved table. As soon as Clint was settled, the servant returned with a pot of mint-scented tea and two fine porcelain cups.

Anticipating Clint's question, Ho spoke first — in precise English. "I am sorry for the deception, Señor Lazo, but a Celestial cannot be too careful in these trying times. I presume you are here in regard to the missing Californio ladies?"

"You know who I am and why I've come?"

"I have heard of you and of your mission. At the risk of seeming less than humble, there is little that goes on, on the river, the bay, or in San Francisco, that I do not hear of. Members of our humble tong are everywhere there are Chinese. The Chinese are already the muscle of California, Señor Lazo. They have ears and many Californio friends among the working class."

"Then you already know why I have come?"

"Yes, and I, too, am concerned with the deception someone has played on both of us. Let me assure you, the Chinese, and certainly those of the Fu Sang Tong, had nothing to do with this."

"How can you be so sure?" Clint settled back in the pillows and sipped the excellent green tea.

"I would swear on the spirits of my ancestors that no Fu Sang member is involved. I would be forever shamed if it were any Chinese, and would wager all the gold of the *gum san* against a farthing that it is not."

"It seems to me that thousands of men without women might have a few among them who would resort to anything — even kidnapping." Clint drained the rest of his tea. "The Anglos will not stand for John Chinaman breaking the law."

"Please do not be offended, Señor Lazo, but I must tell you. You may know something of our language, but you know little about the Celestials."

"Then enlighten me."

Ho stood up and began to pace as he talked. "Do you know why our tong is named Fu Sang?" He didn't wait for an answer. "In your year four hundred and ninety nine, the Buddhist priest Hui Shen, along with other priests, came to the shores of what we Celestials now call *gum san,* the gold mountain. What you Anglos call California." He smiled wryly at Clint. "That, if my history is correct, was long before the Spanish or the Mexicans and was while you Anglos still herded goats in Europe. Hui Shen reported back to the Imperial Court that there was a wondrous tree here, and named the land for that tree, Fu Sang. Its fruit was said to be like pears, its fibers like iron, its root edible. Pins and needles were made from its thorns, paper from its bark, and liquor from its juices."

Clint wondered if he was being fooled. "I know of no tree like that."

"Really?" Ho said, flashing another polite smile. "You've never seen the maguey of Mexico?

"Each year for over a hundred, the Celestials came to the Fu Sang, before we lost interest in a land with no treasure or history, and peopled only by the heathen. If Hui Shen and those who followed him had only gone inland and found the true *gum san,* you, not we, might now be the guest in Fu Sang."

"Hell, maybe the Chinese were here a thousand years before the Spanish. I am a Celt, Zhang Ho, and the Celts, if you know your European history, did more than herd goats. But what does any of this have to do with the problem at hand?"

"I tell you only so you know that the Fu Sang is an old and honorable name, representing an old and honorable people who accomplished much. Still, we know we are here as guests." His tone hardened. "Even though we were here long before the Anglo. We do not complain when you Anglos pass the foreign miner's tax and each Chinese must pay thirty dollars a year to work in the gold fields. We do not complain when you drink your whiskey, act the heathen, and dishonor us by cutting off our queues."

He folded his hands behind his back. "We ship most of what we make back to China, where we all plan to return. The *gum san* is not our home, and as you know, no Chinese wishes to become a citizen of your California. China is our land, as it is the land of our ancestors." He returned to his seat.

"No Chinese did this thing you speak of. The Chinese would not dishonor their homeland, nor their ancestors, by doing such a thing . . . nor would they risk being thrown out

81

of the gold fields."

That made sense to Clint.

Ho sipped the last of his tea. "No, Señor Lazo, the men who did this were not Celestials. All know of the Barracoon. The news flew through California on falcon's wings. Only two weeks ago, the first shipload of *mui gai* arrived. Even now they are overcoming the rigors of the voyage, and within the week will be auctioned off. Soon there will be plenty of Chinese women in San Francisco."

"The Barracoon? *Mui gai?*"

"The Barracoon is the humble place where we, the Fu Sang, will offer indentured Chinese girls, *mui gai,* to any who wish to bid."

"Bid? What the hell is that, Ho? This is a free state."

"It is not slavery, honorable Lazo. It is only the free trading of indentured servants."

"I was indentured, Ho. I know how free an indentured servant is." Clint stood, his fists balled at his sides.

"This sounds like a sham for a slave market to me. The good men of San Francisco will not stand for it."

Ho ignored Clint's remark. "So you see, Señor Lazo, we have no need to abduct Californio women. We will be able to bid for our own very shortly."

Clint walked to the door and pulled it open,

but hesitated a moment. "I don't mean to be rude, honorable Ho. You have been very helpful. I don't think this Barracoon will be the answer to the Celestials' problem. I fear, from what little I know, that it may be just the beginning of a new one. If you hear anything that will help me find the Chi — the abductors of that girl, please contact me."

"It was not the Chinese, honorable Lazo. Look elsewhere. The expensive silk purse sometimes holds the fewest jewels. Look where it is not so obvious. Besides" — Zhang Ho smiled — "if they were Chinese, they would have been clever enough to dress like white devils."

"I'll think on that. Thanks for your help." Clint pulled the door shut, then made his way through the dimly lit barren anteroom and into the street.

He now believed that the abductors were not Chinese. What he knew of Celestials had already given him doubt. And what Zhang Ho had said made sense. If Chinese women were coming to California, or already were there, there would be little reason for the Chinese to risk the wrath of Californians by committing a crime — and it was just not like them. They respected the law.

But still, he felt they were making a mistake with the Barracoon.

CHAPTER SEVEN

"I don't want to move to another room. I want to go home!" Apolonia shouted, and stomped her foot.

Abner Baggs stepped back, hands extended, palms out. "Now, missy, if'n you give me trouble, I'll have to call for some help."

"When do I get to go home?"

"The cap'n will have to talk to you of that. Now, you come on along." He turned and backed down the passageway until he reached the ladder, then pulled a key ring from his belt and worked at the brass lock on a door.

Apolonia eyed the sunlit ladderway behind the old man and wondered if she could manage to run past him; but barefoot, wearing only a smock and not knowing if the ship she was on was at sea or anchored, she hesitated until his attention turned back to her.

"Come on, missy." He pushed open the

door, squinted, and searched the inside until he was satisfied where the others were. "The rest of you step back. Go on, get away from the door." He motioned Apolonia inside, and when she complied, slammed the door behind her. She cringed as she heard the key rattle and the lock being turned.

Relief flooded her as she looked at the others, also barefoot and clad in smocks, in the long, narrow, eight-bunk room. Five other women, three of whom she knew well. Maria Carranda, Helena Obregon, and Señora Juanita Robles rose from their bunks and rushed to her side.

They all began to question her at once, until Juanita Robles hushed them. "Stop it! Stop chattering like barnyard hens." They quieted. Juanita took Apolonia's nervous cold hands. "Are you all right, *niña?* Did they hurt you?"

"I am fine, Señora Robles. My jaw is sore where one of those brutes slapped me . . . an ugly man with a big mustache —"

"Stoddard," Juanita confirmed. "The worst of them."

"And my back and sides are sore. But it is nothing, really. Can you tell me what we are doing here?"

"We know nothing. We hoped you might know what is happening."

For the first time since she had been abducted, Apolonia allowed someone else to see her true feelings. "I am so frightened. . . ." She sank to her knees and began to sob into her hands.

Juanita knelt beside her. "Don't cry, little one. So far, none of us has been hurt . . . or touched in any way."

Apolonia glanced up at Juanita. The thought hadn't yet dawned on her that she might lose her honor. She glanced at the women in the room and realized that they were all beautiful — some of the most beautiful women in northern California — and sobbed even louder.

Juanita rose. "Apolonia Vega, stop crying right this instant," she demanded. Apolonia stopped immediately and looked up at her older friend. She nodded. She would cry no more. Juanita helped her to her feet.

"Either of those top two bunks on the end are yours. The chamber pots are under the lower bunks and there is water in that pitcher."

"How long have you been here?" Apolonia asked, looking from girl to girl, each dressed in a simple straight smock.

"Sarena Gutierez has been here the longest. Almost a week. The rest of us arrived on almost a daily basis."

"Why are we here?" Apolonia's tone rose, and she fought to hold back the tears.

"We just don't know," Juanita said. "Now,

86

kneel with us, and we will pray for guidance."

They sank to their knees and Juanita led them in prayer.

But Apolonia's thoughts were of more immediate problems.

Escape. Somehow they must escape.

Captain Isaac Banyon backed away from the borehole on the wall opposite the one he had used to peek in on Apolonia Vega, and cursed his luck — all of the women were clad. This Vega girl was the most beautiful and the most modest of the women, never removing her smock for any reason. And her modesty caused his neck to tickle with prickly heat and his thick thighs to roast. *Damn her infernal pride.*

Now he had had her placed with the other women. Damnation, he wished they would do something that would give him the excuse to bring them out and punish the papist whores. A sound lashing on their bare backs would serve them. It would break their spirit and their hope for escape, he told himself.

He wished he spoke Spanish. Maybe he would overhear something that would give him the excuse to thrash them. He had some crew members on board who did speak the Mexican tongue, but none of them was among the only five other men who knew of the women.

The sailors had had no problem bringing the *mui gai* from China — willing or unwilling — but they might have a problem concerning the Californio girls, who were clearly opposed to their fate. Some of the sailors on board were probably papists themselves — Banyon had Portuguese and Italians and a Chilean among the crew.

Banyon climbed up the ladder, replaced the floorboards, and stepped out of the closet into his cabin. Lucretia had been taken onshore by his first mate, Stoddard, for some last-minute purchases before they sailed, and would soon return. It wouldn't do to have his wife discover him checking the rudder gear again. She was becoming even more of a problem than usual. He had made a terrible mistake bringing her on this voyage. He brushed the mildewed splinters away from his coat and trousers.

Soon. Soon, he promised himself, he would be able to lay the leather to those comely bare brown backs. Just as he had to a few of those of the heathen litchi-nut-colored China Marys on the trip over. But not so hard as to mark them permanently. Then they would not bring so good a price. Just enough to make them wither and pray to the Lord God Jehova for forgiveness. Wither, and squirm, and kneel before him.

Before Captain Isaac Banyon, and God Jehova.

Clint stopped by the old man's rusted-out boiler shack, left another gold piece, and asked him to find Huly Up Hong. He carefully explained where he would be for the next couple of hours, then worked his way down Calle de Fundación out of Chinatown.

He noted a livery, Hardy's, not far from the saloon he was headed for, and stopped there. He had a belt full of money, but planned to hang on to it. It was for the Kaweah ranch — and San Francisco hotel rates were higher than a cat's back.

"Need a stall for this stallion and a place to bed down, myself," he told the stocky man who met him at the wide doors.

"You're in luck, friend," the man said, extending his hand and introducing himself. He motioned into the darkness of the barn, where a man was saddling a hammer-headed black mule. "That fella is just ridin' out. Normally we're full up."

"I'm real partial to this palomino, Mr. Hardy," Clint cautioned. "See he gets a couple of handfuls of grain a day and a forkful of clean hay. I'd take it personal if I came around and his water bucket was empty."

"We know our job, but I appreciate your

concern. That's a fine-lookin' animal," Hardy said in a businesslike manner. "Your tack and anything else you want to leave will be under lock and key. We don't take responsibility for your goods, but we do our best." He motioned to a walled-in stall with a big brass padlock on it. "Paco!" he yelled to a brown-skinned boy, who ran forward and took Diablo's reins. Then the stocky man strode away toward the rear, with Clint following. "Come on out back and I'll show you a spot."

Clint followed Hardy to the rear of the stable and to a row of rooms that seemed to have been built up against the wall as an afterthought. Each tiny cubicle, half the size of the horse stalls, held a rope-strung log-framed bunk with just enough room beside it to stand and dress.

"You supply your own candle," the stocky man said, "and be damn careful with it. Water is at the trough. Privy is there," and he pointed to an outhouse against a corral fence in the very rear. "Half dollar a day for you and a half dollar for the horse. If your stallion kicks my stalls out or you kick up hell, you're out of here faster than a stump-tailed horse flicks it in flytime."

"Damn." Clint moaned, still trying to reconcile the price.

"If the price or the terms are too steep,

there's a hundred or so who don't think so."

"It'll do," Clint said quickly, knowing he was fortunate to find anything in San Francisco. He handed the man a five-dollar gold piece and gave Paco a few more instructions before he strode out.

"We do a little shoein'," he heard Hardy call after him. "Four bits a shoe with no guarantees." Clint waved over his shoulder.

On the boardwalk in front of the El Dorado, two men leaned against the porch rails, the shorter man reading a newspaper. They straightened as Clint approached, and Clint recognized the redheaded deputy marshal. He searched the man's gaze for any threat, but the green eyes betrayed nothing.

"Hold up a minute, Lazo," the deputy said, his tone, as usual, less than friendly.

"I got a minute, McPherson, but just." Clint's voice was light with a nonchalance he did not really feel.

"This is City Marshal Larson." McPherson motioned to the stocky potbellied man next to him. Two long nine cigars extended out of a pocket of his fancy waistcoat — more that of a gambler than a marshal, Clint thought.

Clint nodded, as the man made no effort to shake. "Did you catch up with that fella who shot the Frenchman?" Clint asked, hoping that was the reason he had been summoned.

Larson pulled out one of his cigars and shoved it in his mouth. McPherson snatched a match from his own pocket and lit his boss's long nine. Larson blew a cloud of smoke before he answered for his deputy.

"We caught up with him, and he and six other witnesses testified it was a fair fight. You and that Negra gonna find any fault with that?"

"Not really my business," Clint said. "Can't speak for Mr. LaMont, but it'd be my guess he's got other rows to hoe."

"Good thing," Larson said smugly. "I'd hate for the newspaper" — he shook a rolled-up copy of the *San Francisco Call* at Clint — "to get the wrong impression about the way we handle our business. The *Call* is itchin' to find some dirt to kick up."

" 'Course, nobody would pay no mind to what that Negro said anyways," McPherson said. "That's all, Lazo." The deputy turned his back on Clint.

"Not quite all." Clint fished into his pocket and came up with the picture of Apolonia Vega. "This young lady is missing and her father has asked me to make the law aware of it."

"Right good-lookin' woman, for a greaser,"

Larson said, a slow smile curling his lips and puffing the cheeks of his round face. McPherson reached for the picture, but Clint repocketed it. He fought an impulse to shove the cigar down the potbellied marshal's throat.

"She's missing" — Clint managed to keep his voice steady — "and I understand a number of other Californio girls are too."

"I've had two families in my office expecting me to search for these women." Larson took a deep draw on his cigar and exhaled. "We got no time to look for runaway girls. That's a family matter."

"Runaway? Apolonia Vega was abducted. Carried off by the Chinese, or at least by men dressed as Chinese. Eyewitness said so."

"The Vega place is way up the river, ain't it, Ryan?" the marshal snapped.

"Halfway to Sacramento City," McPherson chimed in.

"Way out of my jurisdiction," the marshal said with a politician's smile. "I've got enough trouble right here in San Francisco. Don't have to go lookin' for other people's, particularly foreigners'."

How right you are, Don Vega, Clint thought. "If you happen to hear of anything, I would appreciate knowing about it," Clint said, still fighting to keep his temper.

"You some kind of lawman?" McPherson

asked, raising an eyebrow.

"Nope," Clint said quickly. "Family asked me to see if I can locate their daughter."

"Keeping an eye out is one thing," Larson said. "Trying to play lawman is another. Don't you be breaking the law while you're sticking your nose into the law's business. We're trying to keep the peace with the Chinese, and we don't need strangers coming around stirrin' things up."

"If the law took this Vega matter on as their business, the Vegas wouldn't have to hire someone," Clint snapped.

"I offered that as a suggestion," Larson said. He took a half step forward, all trace of a smile gone from his face. "Now take it as a warning, Lazo, if that's really your name. Don't break the law, or the law'll break you."

"I wouldn't think of it, Marshal," Clint said, his voice steady and assured, but his blood boiling. Clint tipped his hat, trying to convert the smirk on his face into a smile, but it didn't quite work. He turned on his heel, headed away, and shoved through the batwing doors.

Larson stared after him, gnawing on the long nine. "I don't much like that som'bitch," he said, more to himself than to his deputy. He glanced at McPherson. "You nose around and find out what you can about this Lazo. That's a funny handle for a man who sounds like he's from New England."

Clint shoved through the crowd in the El Dorado. It was strangely silent. Then he realized why. Ostrich-feathered bulging-bodiced Sultana Mulvany had taken the stage.

A pianoforte player with a head as white and clean of hair as his ivory keys sat at an upright just below the stage. Where a New York pianist might have his sheet music, a sawed-off scattergun rested in a buckhorn rack. Clint smiled, figuring the cigar-smoking ivory tinkler had duties other than his music — such as keeping the rowdy bunch from laying their hands on Sultry, the Barbary Warbler, as she was rapidly becoming known.

The room fell so silent Clint could hear beer-foam bubbles bursting in the mugs. The first notes of "My Old Kentucky Home" brought cheers from half a dozen in the room, but they were quickly quelled by threats of lost life from those who wanted to hear every tone and inflection of the feminine voice. The men stood in respectful silence until she finished. Then the place rocked and dust rose with foot-stomping hand-pounding enthusiasm.

During the uproar, Clint elbowed his way to the bar and muscled in between a miner and a black-suited high-hatted Negro dude. He smiled as he noted that the suit had been let out with inset swatches of bright red cloth. A four-inch-wide patch ran down the middle of the back of the coat, and two-inch stripes down the outside of each leg converged in the seat of the pants and ran upward to the waist. A gold-handled walking stick hung from the brass-edged bar.

"By the saints!" Clint exclaimed when he focused on the man's dusky face. "If it isn't Gideon LaMont."

Turning his eyes from the stage, where Sultry was waving as she left and the piano player was scrambling around gathering tossed gold coins, Gideon flashed a grin and extended his large, rosy-palmed hand. "At your service, sir."

Clint pumped it.

"I'd be proud to buy you a drink, Mr. Ryan." Gideon quietly motioned the barman over.

"I would accept, sir," Clint said, still amused at the costume. "I see you decided not to bury your unfortunate friend in his city suit."

"No sense in soiling such a fine piece of goods when I could find a talented Chinaman to resurrect it." Gideon placed a gold piece on the bar and paid for Clint's whiskey. "Unfortunately" — Gideon smiled playfully — "he had no black cloth."

"It appears you have prospered since I last

saw you," Clint said with a wry smile as Gideon swept his change from the bar.

Gideon leaned closer to Clint and spoke in low tones. "It seems that Henri LaMont carried a money belt with a considerable amount of gold. I would not have found it, had I not decided that he would no longer be in need of the suit. I relieved him of what I felt was a fair wage, after found, for thirty-three years of service, and entrusted Adam's Express Company with the balance."

He took a deep draw on his flavored soda water. "It, and a note informing them that I consider myself a freedman, since California is surely coming into the Union as a free state, is even now on its way to New Orleans and the LaMont family."

"Sounds fair enough to me," Clint said, but he couldn't contain a chuckle.

"Quiet!" The miner on the other side of him cautioned with a hard tone when Sultry returned to the stage. The piano tinkled and she began to work her way through a lively "Camptown Races."

She finished her number and fled the stage. Gold and silver coins rained down on it from the enthusiastic crowd. The pianoforte player/bodyguard scrambled over the stage collecting the money. The place resumed its midrange roar. Men returned to gambling, drinking, laughing, and telling lies about the amount of gold in the hills — but a few of them proved it by the number of nuggets they piled on the gambling tables.

Clint quietly related his business to Gideon, who listened with interest.

"This Barracoon," Gideon said, his face strained and distant, "sounds no better than the slave auctions of the South."

"I agree," Clint said. "But it appears this, too, is legal. Indenture contracts have long been bought and sold . . . even in the free states."

"Doesn't make it right. Do you think it has anything to do with the missing Californio girl?"

"I don't know. But rotten apples tend to rest in the same barrel, and dealers of women . . . Hell, I'm just guessing, but I don't have anything else to go on. Those women could be somewhere in the Sierras by now, or on their way to Mexico, or the territories, or who knows where."

"So what now?"

"I'm waiting for a man who can help me find this Barracoon. I'm gonna see for myself what it's all about."

He had just finished his statement when someone tapped his shoulder. He turned to look down into the wide face of Huly Up Hong.

Clint dug into his pocket, found a couple of silver pesos, and placed them in Hong's palm. "This is for finding Mr. Ho for me. And this" — he flashed another five-dollar gold piece — "is for taking me to the Barracoon and getting me inside."

Huly Up's eyes flared, and he glanced quickly around. He shook his head, and his long black queue, protruding through a black skullcap, danced. "No do. Not possible. No."

Clint eyed him and the men around them, standing almost shoulder to shoulder. "Come on outside. We'll talk there."

Gideon drained his mug of soda water and followed.

They walked outside, now in darkness, and Clint led the way to a nearby alley. "Now, why the hell can't you take me to the Barracoon?"

"General Zhang Ho cut my throat if interfere in his business."

"General? Ho is a general?"

"He led revolt against emperor. He is vely powerful man in China. Vely powerful man here in *gum san*."

"Come on, Hong, no one will know if you just show me where it is."

"Everyone know soon. In two days, auction."

"I want to know now. Five dollars gold."

Huly Up's eyes narrowed. "You tell no one?"

"Not even my sainted mother." Clint smiled.

"Midnight. I take you there midnight."

"You'll take *us* there," Gideon said, speaking for the first time.

"Ten dollar, take two."

"Is it farther if you take two?" Gideon asked with a hard look.

"More risk."

"Not with me." Gideon grinned wryly. "Can't see me in the dark."

Clint smiled, but Hong obviously didn't see the humor.

"White devil mad at John Chinaman," Hong said with a grimace, "then Chinaman lose honorable queue. Chinaman mad at Chinaman, then Chinaman lose queue and head 'long with it. Seven dollar fifty cent," he offered.

"Six dollars even," Gideon said, not losing his grin. To Clint's surprise he pulled the walking stick open slightly, exposing a gleaming blade hidden in its shaft.

"Six dollar," Hong agreed quickly, "but no wait to show you way back."

"I've never been anywhere I couldn't find my way back from," Gideon said, and winked at Clint.

"Be here, midnight, no wait. Huly Up always on time." Hong shuffled away and disappeared down the alley.

CHAPTER
EIGHT

"I'll hang those bloody fools until the gulls pick their bones clean!" Isaac Banyon roared. Harlan Stoddard took a step back, his large bulk cowering before the verbal onslaught. "Had ye been minding the quarterdeck as ye should, 'twould not have happened."

"Those gold-hungry fools must have gone down the forward anchor rode, Cap'n." Harlan nervously smoothed down his thick mustache with the palm of his hand. "Prob'ly had a boat waitin'. I was alert, sir. But a man can't be everywhere."

"Five men. Five experienced crewmen we have to replace. Hear me, Harlan Stoddard. You'll be a common seaman again if ye don't get me a full crew in less than a week. We sail then, and by the gods of the sea, you'll be pullin' double shifts on the yardarms if ye don't have those men replaced."

Stoddard's gut ached from the captain's harangue. How the hell could he be expected to watch the whole damned crew? More than eight hundred ships lay at anchor in San Francisco Harbor, each shy of sailors, each swaying on the tide, her fo'c'sle empty, her men in the Sierras seeking the golden metal that had brought their ships there in the first place.

"We'd do well not to lose more afore we sail, Cap'n Banyon," Stoddard said quietly, steeling his resolve not to take all the blame for the desertion.

"Belay that!" Banyon shouted, spittle flying. "Shanghai me a crew, or we'll sail shorthanded and I'll put the papist wenches on the ratlines with you."

"I'll do me best," Stoddard said, "but it'll not be easy. Every bloody man in San Francisco is armed to the teeth, and there be few drunks. They come, provision up, and set off for the mountains."

"White, yellow, brown, or black, Stoddard. A crew. A full crew in five days or I'll feed your mate's papers to the fishes."

"You'll have your crew, Cap'n," Stoddard agreed, but as he turned and descended the ladder off the dark quarterdeck, he wondered how the hell he would accomplish such an impossible task. If he didn't have a crew in five days, he decided, he would join the other men

102

in the Sierras. Hell, who needed the abuse of this crazy captain? Who needed first mate's papers if he had his pockets full of gold?

With gold, he could buy his own bloody ship. The harbor was full of them.

Clint reached over, plucked Gideon's pocket watch from his waistcoat, and checked the time. In half an hour they were to meet Huly Up. Clint had sipped only beer while they waited, wanting to be alert when he visited the Barracoon. He had no idea what he would find, or really even why he thought he should go there. It was merely his hunter's instinct, but he had learned to follow it.

"Are you headin' for the gold fields, mate?" A thin-faced man no taller than Clint's shoulder asked as he elbowed his way to the bar next to him.

"Thought I might, in a few days," Clint answered.

"Then I'm just the bloke you need." He smiled a crooked grin and focused both a good and a wandering eye on Clint.

"I didn't know I needed a bloke." Clint instinctively rested his hand on the pouch of gold he carried laced through his gun belt. He had heard about the Sydney Ducks, and this man's accent identified him as one. On the Barbary Coast, they were among the most feared of all the ethnic groups.

"It's not a man you need, mate, but a map. I've been to the fields, mate, and made me poke . . . enough to last me the rest of me life. I'm headin' out for home on the first outbound vessel. You look like a good enough sort, and I'll not be needing me mountain of gold any longer. I've got more'n a man can carry." He glanced from side to side to make sure no one was listening.

"Reginald Shaddock's me handle." He extended a thin hand, and Clint felt as if he were about to have his pocket picked, but he shook and introduced himself. "Are you in the market for a map to a hill o' gold?" Shaddock continued.

"I thought you said a mountain." Clint couldn't help but smile.

"Hill, mountain, who's to quibble? It's more than either of us could spend if we lived five lifetimes. That's the reason I've left it and headed home. Got more'n I can spend."

A few steps away, Gideon turned from the faro game he was watching and stepped over beside Clint. "Fish, Mr. Ryan is a friend of mine and knows California from the sea to the desert. Sell your maps to the pilgrims."

"Well, if it isn't me abo mate, Gideon." Reginald "Fish" Shaddock managed to focus both eyes on Gideon. "Since you're not in the market for the opportunity of a lifetime, how 'bout standing a mate to a mug?"

Clint laughed and Gideon motioned to the bartender for a beer. For a man with a mountain of gold, this Sydney Duck was quick to skate a drink.

The same bulldog bartender who had given Clint a bad time the first time he was in the El Dorado slammed the mug of Dog's Head bass ale down in front of the Australian.

"Drink your Dog's Head, Fish, and keep your hands in your own pockets. I'll be having no trouble tonight."

Fish nodded. "You'll have no trouble from me, Luther Baggs," he said, and drained the mug in one long gulping swallow. He backhanded the foam from his mouth and turned back to Clint. "So you're a native?"

"Compared to most. I've been here over three years."

"I know a body in need of a guide and a bodyguard, if you be handy with those weapons." The Aussie glanced at the Colt revolver at Clint's waist and the rifle leaning against the bar.

"Handy enough."

"Would there be a commission in it for an agent who brought you a job — say, ten percent?" Fish's eye wandered, giving him the wary look of a darting haddock who kept a constant bulging eye out for the shark.

"I guess, Mr. Fish, if I took a job I'd be happy to pay a commission," Clint agreed, though he had no intention of taking one.

"Good enough," Shaddock said, and disappeared into the crowd.

Gideon rested a hand on Clint's shoulder. "He's a slippery one, that Fish. He'd snatch the pennies off a dead man's eyes."

"I'll keep mine open," Clint said. Gideon nodded, then returned to watching the game.

Fish returned almost as quickly as he had disappeared, with the bald-headed piano player in tow. "Now, you two blokes don't be forgettin' that I'm in this for a commission."

Ignoring Fish, the bald-headed man, whose eyebrows were bushy enough to make up for his clean pate, removed a stubby cigar from his scowling mouth, spat a chunk at a nearby spittoon, missed, and extended his hand to Clint.

"Jasper Henry," he said, and Clint shook with him, noting with amazement his stubby fingers and thick hands. He got the impression that even the knots on his bald head were muscles. "Fish tells me you're a man who knows every nook and cranny of California and can hit a gnat at a hundred yards with that Colt's."

"The only thing Fish knows about me is that I'm not in the market for his gold mountain map."

"Then he's wasting our time." Jasper Henry shoved the cigar stub back in his mouth and turned to leave.

"Wait, now," Fish said, seeing his commission flying away. "I'm as good a judge of character as any man. Can you?" he asked.

"Can I what?" Clint smiled.

"Can you hit a gnat at a hundred yards with that fancy revolving Colt's?" Jasper eyed Clint's Californio clothes and awaited the answer with furrowed eyebrows.

"I doubt a gnat. Maybe a big green horsefly," Clint said, "if you mean on the wing." He laughed heartily.

"See, I told you, Jasper. And he knows every rock and tree in California."

"Is that true?"

"I know southern California and the coast south of San Francisco. I've been up the Kaweah into the Sierras, but those mountains are big enough it would take a man a lifetime to know them. I've been through the Ton Tache, but no white man knows it well."

"How about the gold country?" Jasper asked anxiously.

"Never had the pleasure," Clint answered honestly.

Gideon, bored with the faro game, turned to listen in.

"Then you're no good to me," Jasper said gruffly.

Clint was becoming a little irritated with the man's manner. "I never said I was *anything* to you, friend."

Fish stepped between the two men. "You'll not find a man around here who knows much about the gold country, Jasper. Hell, the ones what found gold are still there and the ones what didn't are pushin' on, still lookin'. You need a man that knows his way around, and this here's your bloke. Right, Ryan?"

"I've never been anywhere I couldn't find my way back from," Clint said. He winked at Gideon, who chuckled.

"You might just do. I'll talk to my boss." Jasper started to turn just as the crowd behind him parted and Sultry Mulvany floated up. Clint snatched his broad-brimmed, sand-colored hat off his head and Gideon had his narrow-brimmed high hat in hand as quickly.

"This is Miss Sultana Mulvany," Jasper said. Clint bowed slightly.

"And this is my friend, Gideon LaMont," Clint said.

"Pleased, I'm sure," she said, extending her hand. Gideon bowed deeply, a little surprised at the white woman's reaction. He accepted the hand and brushed it near his lips.

"*Enchanté, Mademoiselle,*" Gideon said in perfect French. Sultana beamed.

"Why, it's so nice to meet a true gentleman," she said, and Gideon's status in San Francisco was elevated to the zenith. The nearby crowd buzzed.

"I've been speaking to Mr. Ryan about employment," Jasper said, stepping between Gideon and his employer, obviously irritated by her reaction to the black man.

"Are you considering joining us on our trek to the gold country, Mr. Ryan?" Her voice rang as only a trained singer's would.

"You're to become an argonaut, too, Miss Mulvany?"

"No, sir." She laughed, and the sound of it enchanted those in the room close enough to hear. "I'm only going to mine the miners, so to speak. Singing is my business, and the whole world is my stage. I plan to have a traveling road show."

"I'm afraid I'm currently employed. And soon, with luck, I'll have a herd of horses to drive south."

"Damn," Fish muttered under his breath. He looked accusingly at a miner nearby as if he had been the one disrespectful enough to mutter a curse in front of Sultana Mulvany.

"I'm sorry to hear that," she said, looking Clint up and down with obvious admiration. "I don't doubt your qualifications, and am in need of a skilled guide and guard."

"Maybe next time," Clint said, and every man within earshot moaned.

"It's been a pleasure," she said. Clint sensed a hint of disappointment as her liquid blue eyes darkened for a second. "Gentlemen." She flashed a brilliant smile and turned. The crowd parted as she moved away, and both Clint and Gideon returned their hats to their heads.

"Damned fool," Clint heard a man exclaim, and several more agreed.

Sensing there was no money to be made, and seeing no purses easily lifted, Fish slipped off into the crowd.

"As God is my witness," Gideon said with conviction, "that's the most beautiful creature on this earth. Her hand was like a feather in mine. Hair like corn silk, eyes as blue as the Caribbean, and skin as smooth and clean as crystal glass."

"Never truer words," Clint said as he watched her ascend the stairs next to the stage and disappear behind the curtain. Following his employer, Jasper Henry paused and glared back at Clint. Clint held his gaze until Jasper turned and disappeared behind the curtain.

"What time is it, Gideon?" Clint asked.

The broad-shouldered man checked his pocket watch.

"It's almost midnight."

"Then let's go find Huly Up."

They elbowed their way out of the El Dorado.

CHAPTER NINE

True to his word and the six dollars in gold, Huly Up Hong waited in the alley.

"How far?" Clint asked.

"Few blocks. Near bottom of Telegraph Hill." Huly Up trudged off, his black pants flapping, his sandals slapping callused heels, and his long queue bouncing. Clint toted the Colt's revolving rifle and followed behind Gideon and Huly Up. He would rather carry the long gun than trust anyone with it. He had seen too many admiring glances since he had been in San Francisco.

Soon the planked streets gave way to dirt, and lantern-lit windows to dark shuttered ones. He remembered thinking that Chinatown must be the best-lit place in the city with all the paper lanterns. He was wrong, for though there were many lanterns, only very few were lit. Huly Up's pace slowed and soon he was walking a few steps and stopping to glance in each nook and alleyway.

"It would not do to be seen," he whispered. On a dark street lined with shanties, he stopped at an alleyway. "Alley only go partway. At end is door to Barracoon. Guard at door, guard at windows on side street."

Clint dug in his pocket and fished out the five-dollar gold piece and a one-dollar one and handed it to the Chinese.

"I pay my own way," Gideon whispered.

"You buy the drinks when we get back to the El Dorado," Clint said, and caught the flash of Gideon's smile.

"Hope you get back," Huly Up whispered, then turned and disappeared down the street.

Clint and Gideon crossed the alley, carefully surveying it, but it was too dark to see. They rounded the corner, walking with a purposeful stride, as if they had a destination. A guard rose as they neared, backed into a deep doorway, and gripped a long tong ax. They ignored him and hurried on.

The Barracoon was a two-story clapboard building set exactly in the middle of the block. It extended to one side street, was lined with closed shops on the opposite street, and the alley dead-ended into it front and back.

"How many of these China girls do they have in that place?" Gideon asked.

"I have no idea, but if they're going to have an auction, there must be plenty."

"You gonna knock on the door, or do you have something else in mind?"

"By the scowl on that guard's face, I don't think knocking on the door in the dark of night is exactly the right approach." Clint scanned the dark street. The fog was beginning to settle in, so he could only see a half block in the darkness. "If we wait awhile, this fog may cover anything we want to do. If we climb to the roof of these shops, I bet we'll find a way into the second story."

"Makes sense to me. And odds are, the later we wait, the more chance of the guards dozin' off."

They settled back against a shuttered shack and waited. By the end of the first half hour, the fog was so thick Clint could barely see the foresights of the Colt's rifle if he held it out in front of him. They crossed the street and found a likely porch fronting one of the more permanent shops. Linking his fingers, Gideon boosted Clint up, then handed up his rifle. Clint reached down and clasped wrists with Gideon, hoisting him up. In a moment they were creeping across the flat *brea*-mopped roof of a Chinese shop. They came upon the second-story wall of the Barracoon almost before they saw it.

Clint felt his way to a rough wooden shutter. He leaned his Colt's rifle against the wall, unsheathed a short-bladed knife and ran the blade up and down between the center crack until he found the latch, and tripped the simple mechanism. The shutter swung outward. The room was dark as a foot up a bull's backside, and smelled somewhat worse. Clint swung over the sill and entered. He drew a sulfurhead across the horn shank of his knife and it flared, lighting the room with a dull flickering glow.

"A storage room," he whispered, and Gideon followed him inside. Clint moved across the room, its shelves filled with cartons and bales and bottles of exotic substances that Clint had never seen. Each was identified with Chinese characters.

Quietly, a quarter inch at a time, he opened the door.

Voices startled him. The building was open in the center, the roof in that area two stories high. Surrounding the fifty-by-fifty-foot center court was a railed walkway with rooms off it. In the open area below, on a raised platform two feet higher than the rest of the floor, several Chinese surrounded a table lit by a single whale-oil lantern. Long-handled tong hatchets hung from their waists or leaned against chairs. One man wore a broad-bladed sword that caught the light of the lantern.

They shouted and moaned as they played fan-tan.

The raised area must be the auction floor, Clint thought as he moved quietly down the walk-way. *It would make a good place to show off the goods.* It was almost pitch-dark above the hooded lantern and if he made no noise there was no reason the nine men he counted below would know of his presence. The first door he came to was barred from the outside. It wouldn't be, he reasoned, unless they wanted to keep something in. He carefully worked the bar away, just as Gideon caught up with him.

With a loud squeak, the door opened. The noise from the men below quieted. Neither Clint nor Gideon breathed as they awaited footfalls on the stairway leading to the walk-way. But they didn't come. The men returned to their game, their singsong chatter reassuring.

Clint eased inside and Gideon followed, leaving the door slightly ajar so they might have a chance of hearing approaching foot-steps. They stood perfectly still, waiting for eyes to adjust.

A fine ray of light filtered through the crack in the open door, and Clint could make out the open, fear-filled eyes of a girl lying in a bunk, staring back.

He sensed that there were other girls in the room, but could only make out what appeared to be built-in bunks. He moved forward to the girl, who whimpered something in Chinese that Clint didn't understand. He knelt beside the bed. "I'm not going to hurt you," he said, dredging up his best Chinese.

She gaped at him in surprise, then swung her feet out of the bunk and stood. Clint rose to face her. Her hair was intricately braided and piled on top of her head, making her almost as tall as Clint. He couldn't help but glance down — even in the darkness he could make out the proud breasts that pushed against the silk wrapper she wore.

"You speak the language of the Celestials?" she asked.

"I am an ignorant man, beautiful girl, but I try," he said with his finest Chinese humility.

"Why are you here?"

"To see that everything is all right with the China girls." He smiled.

Her eyes cut to the doorway. "Do they know you are here?"

"No. I have come without their knowledge." Clint struggled with the words, but she understood.

She stepped forward, stumbled, and caught herself against his chest. Only then did Clint realize that her feet had been bound, allowed to grow into little more than stubs on the ends of her slender legs. He had seen it before on a Chinese girl in the Sandwich Islands and knew that the Celestials found it beautiful. He found it barbaric.

"You will buy Su Chin?"

Slightly taken aback, Clint changed the subject. "Are there other girls here? Mexican girls?"

"What is Mexican?" she asked.

"Are there girls here who are not Chinese?"

"Only China girls, and Su Chin is the most beautiful."

Looking at her, Clint had no reason to doubt her words, nor the quiet desperation with which they were offered.

"You buy Su Chin's contract?" she pressed.

"You will bring a very high price," Clint complimented her. She smiled slightly, but sadly, he thought.

"I hate this." Gideon spoke for the first time. "Let's herd these women out of here and turn them loose."

"Hell, Gideon, I don't even know if they want to be turned loose, and in case you didn't notice, there's about two thousand pounds of Chinese-mean down below. Let's get the hell out of here. I've learned what I came to learn."

Gideon began to pull the door open, but heard the approach of footsteps. Pausing only an instant, he opened it wider and snatched up the two-by-four used to bar it. The burly guard's eyes flared in surprise at the tall black man in the patched city suit whose hat barely cleared the doorway.

He who hesitates is lost, Gideon figured, and drove the end of the two-by-four deep into the man's midsection.

The man *oofed* loudly and doubled.

"Come on!" Gideon yelled, and brought the other end of the bar across the back of the man's head, felling him.

"Please buy Su Chin," the girl called after Clint, who scrambled through the door and followed Gideon down the walkway at a pounding run.

Gideon darted through the storeroom door before Clint reached it. Realizing a half dozen men were almost to the top of the stairs, Clint took two quick steps in their direction and planted a booted foot in the chest of the first man to top the stairs and kicked hard.

The guard threw up his arms and tumbled, gathering the others as he fell. They went down the stairway in a screaming pile. Clint scrambled through the storeroom and dived out the window, where Gideon pulled him to his feet. He grabbed his rifle from its resting place, and they flew off the rooftop onto the porch roof and hit the ground at a run. It was so dark and foggy they could have hidden five feet from their pursuers and not have been seen.

Instead, they ran for half a block, then began to walk.

"Where the hell are we?" Clint asked, puffing, his breath short in the cold night air and from the rush of excitement.

"Be damned if I know," Gideon said, also puffing.

"Hell," Clint said, "and you're the fellow who can find his way back from anywhere he's been?"

"I can, and I will, as soon as this soup clears."

"It would take a ship's compass to get us home," Clint grumbled.

"Then let's find a place to curl up and lay low."

"I think I'd rather be curled up in that room full of China Marys."

"As would I, my friend," Gideon agreed, "but only if they were free. I'd as soon lay with a goat than with a woman who was not there of her own free will."

"Well said, my friend, and I agree."

"Good. Now let's find a hole for a while."

CHAPTER TEN

Gaspar Cota reined the big bay stallion sharply around and impatiently awaited his three vaqueros.

The waterfront street teemed with work wagons loaded with lumber and produce, argonauts and Chinese just off the ships and still agog at the hustle and bustle — or staring at the road, expecting to pick up nuggets of gold — and a few workmen who had not yet earned their stake so they could leave for the diggin's. Trace chains clanked and wheels and axles creaked as whips cracked their twenty-foot braided rawhide namesakes and cursed their stock. Creaking along, a *careta* filled with stiff cowhides and pulled by two lumbering oxen paused before a herd of swine. The pigs squealed and snorted and rooted in the road while a pair of homespun-clad boys moved them along with the help of stout willow switches and a yapping yellow dog. A farmer in a wide-brimmed straw hat shouted orders to them from astride a deep-chested roman-nosed dray horse while trying to keep the two dozen, slaughterhouse-bound, black and white hogs from being scattered in the traffic. The farmer tipped his straw to the Californio in the *careta*, who doffed his sombrero in return.

But one ingredient necessary to make the burgeoning town into a city was painfully absent from the scene — women. Not one skirt — just a smattering of long robes worn by some male Chinese immigrants.

The vaqueros caught up with their patron's son. Although each of the other vaqueros had some silver trim on his tack, Gaspar was a picture of the fancy Californio don, with silver conchas covering head-stall, martingale, and saddle. The fenders and tapaderos of the high-canted saddle were completely layered with two-inch-square engraved silver plates that caught the sun and announced his arrival with glittering magnificence, and Gaspar, in wide embroidered sombrero, silver concha-festooned vest, and fancy *calzonevas*, drew the attention of every Sydney Duck in this section of the Barbary Coast.

Fish Shaddock leaned on a rough adz-hewn oak hitching post among five of his fellow Australians, eyeing the riders, mentally calculating the weight of the silver trim along with the horses' value. The four Californios worked their way out of the clatter of drays and wagons.

"Have ya ever seen such a fancy bloke?" Fish murmured, a slow smile curling one side of his mouth as he crammed a cigarillo into the other.

"Never in all my days," Booker Whittle's gravelly voice reverberated behind Fish. He wheezed as he sucked in a breath.

As the gods tend to be, they had been unfair when they had divided the attributes between these two men. Where Fish lacked size and power, Booker more than made up for it, with arms the size of most men's thighs and a neck like a bull. Where Booker lacked brains and cunning, Fish was more than adequate. Together, they were a dangerous pair.

"Shall I bang their heads together, Fish?" Booker asked with considerable enthusiasm. He spat a stream of tobacco juice into the dust, dug into his pocket, and gnawed another chaw from a twist.

Fish turned and eyed his barrel-chested companion, who looked as if his face had been used as a butcher's block. Eyebrows sagged from going unstitched after being battered, giving the big man a constant glaring grimace.

Cauliflowered ears bulged from a too-round head and framed a pudgy face scarred and mangled from a hundred fights in as many waterfront taverns all over the Pacific. Booker had a habit of running his tongue through the gap left when a front and canine tooth had succumbed to a belaying pin during a shipboard brawl.

He wheezed when he spoke, as air no longer traversed his bent and angled nose, flattened to twice its original width. All of it combined to give Booker Whittle the glowering look and sound of a mastiff, and he imparted the same powerful presence when he was in a room. More so in the back alleys he and Fish frequented.

"Let's sit a bit and see what they're up to, mate," Fish said as he watched the vaqueros approach.

Gaspar's mount pranced and sidestepped as he reined up in front of the Outback Roo, the waterfront Australian hangout, and dismounted. His vaqueros aligned their stallions at the rail, then followed their patron's son through the batwing doors of the clapboard building. The Roo's entrance featured carved kangaroos decorating the jambs on either side. Its two tall thin windows, bracketing the batwings, faced the daytime hustle and bustle and nighttime threat of Front Street, and its rear door rested well out upon Peabody's Wharf — far enough into the bay that the Roo boasted indoor privies which deposited processed beer directly into the surging bay twenty feet below.

The Roo was the thirteenth saloon Gaspar and his vaqueros had visited in the two days they had been in San Francisco, but so far they had learned nothing about Californio girls being abducted by Chinese. Worse, their meanderings through Chinatown were a study in frustration, since none of them spoke Chinese, and none of the Chinese they met spoke Spanish. Smiles and polite nods were the best they had gotten.

Gaspar was a little drunk, somewhat frustrated, and a whole lot angry. As he led his men inside the saloon, his nose twitched in rebellion at the odor of sweaty men and cigar smoke. He kicked through sawdust and peanut shells, his big roweled spurs clanking, and made his way up to the bar.

"A gift from the gods, mate," Fish said, flipping his cigar butt in the dust and leading Booker into the saloon behind the four vaqueros. "A bloody gift from the gods."

Fish quickly surveyed the twenty or so occupants of the dim smoke-filled establishment. By far the majority of the customers were other Australians, men who would have been on their way to the diggin's if they had not been without the money to buy grub and picks and shovels. Men who would do almost anything to get those necessities. Most of them drank little due to their economic situation — dead broke. They just sat and groused about their fate and awaited an opportunity to change it.

Satisfied that he was among friends and possible co-conspirators, and followed by the toughest of all the Ducks, Fish moved confidently alongside the vaqueros who stood side by side at the long plank bar. Mugs of *aguardiente* sat in front of the men.

"Beer, mate," Fish instructed the bartender.

"I thought you said you were shy of money," Booker complained, looking accusingly at his slight friend and running his tongue in and out of the space between his teeth.

"Out of knock-about money, mate. This is business." Satisfied with that, Booker upended his beer mug, leaving a dollop of foam adorning his bent nose. Fish let his mug rest on the bar and nudged the vaquero next to him. "What brings you fellows down out of the bush?" he asked, a crocodile smile curving his mouth.

The vaquero looked at him coldly, then said something in Spanish to the fancily dressed dude who had ridden the silver-studded saddle, and stepped aside to let his *jefe,* his boss, speak to Fish.

"Have you been here long, amigo?" Gaspar asked in English while he tried to decide which of Fish's eyes to focus on.

"Here? Here in the Roo?" Fish asked in return.

"Here in San Francisco." Gaspar's tone was short, his attitude superior.

I'll soon cure the fancy-pants dude of his snotty airs, Fish thought, but did not misplace his smile. "I've been in Frisco since the beginning, mate," he said proudly. "Ol' Fish knows every nook and cranny, every back alley and Barbary Coast brothel. You fellas here looking to take a meander up cock alley?"

Gaspar ignored the question and eyed the little Sydney Duck as if he were a rat in the kitchen grain bin. The pox was the last thing he wanted, and the only brothels on the waterfront were full of pox-ridden Peruvian girls. Even they were in such demand that the lines extended for a block.

"Since the beginning!" Gaspar retorted with a smirk. "You were here when Mission Dolores began a hundred years ago?"

"No, friend, when the rush began." Fish's lips curled again in a smile, but his eyes held contempt. "When the real Frisco began. Are

127

ya looking to find a little recreation?"

"I am seeking information."

"Then you come to the right place, friend."

"How do you know that, when you don't know what it is I seek?" Gaspar glared down at the smaller man.

"Just tell ol' Fish your problem, and I guarantee I'm your man."

Gaspar's knuckles tightened on the mug. Had it been another time and place, he w〟uld have had this runt of a man horsewhipped for his audacity, but Gaspar had a family matter to solve, a matter of pride.

"I seek information. We have had a señorita abducted and a vaquero killed by some Chinese scum. I will pay in gold coin" — he tapped a pocket — "to find them so they can be punished, and even more to find Señorita Apolonia Vega."

A gift from the gods, Fish thought. "Best we take a seat at a table away from the rest. As I said, I'm your man. Ol' Fish knows the Chine'e like the back of his hand."

For the first time in two days, Gaspar felt a glimmer of hope. He managed a knife-edged smile and turned to a slender vaquero at the bar.

"Be alert, Chato. This is a place to watch your back." Chato Juarez, Gaspar's head vaquero, merely nodded, and continued his vigil and his drink.

Gaspar moved away to a vacant table. Fish lingered to give quiet instructions to Booker, repeated them to make sure he had them, then flashed his crocodile grin at Gaspar and trailed him across the sawdust floor.

As Gaspar and Fish talked quietly, Booker moved to the end of the bar to whisper with the bartender. Then from table to table he quietly negotiated in his no-choice manner with the Sydney Ducks seated there.

To the vaqueros' pleasant surprise, Fish graciously paid for the next round of *aguardiente*. Gaspar drank and told his tale and had almost decided he had been mistaken about the little man when he realized he was becoming dizzy. The Ducks didn't wait for the drinks to take their full effect. As Gaspar rose unsteadily from his chair and called out to his vaqueros, the Aussies fell upon them.

The drugged and dazed vaqueros were no match for the twenty Ducks. Mugs and fists crashed against heads, and sombreros rolled into the sawdust. A few well-placed blows and Gaspar and his men, beaten into unconsciousness, sprawled on the floor, trussed, gagged, and blindfolded. Passersby glanced inside but made no effort to interfere in what was a common occurrence on the Barbary Coast. With a smile of triumph, Fish dug into Gaspar's pocket and found his poke full of gold and silver coin and distributed the money among the Ducks — with three shares going to the bartender, whose laudanum had been used.

Booker flung Gaspar over his shoulder while other Ducks dragged his three vaqueros to the rear of the saloon. Booker creaked open a gaping trapdoor in the plank floor. The longboat heaving in the waves below would hold eight men comfortably.

With little ceremony the vaqueros were roughly lowered and loaded like so many trussed goats on their way to market.

CHAPTER
ELEVEN

Clint and Gideon spent the morning in Chinatown. They moved from shop to shop, asking
questions. Even though Clint spoke enough
of the language to get by, he remained frustrated by his lack of progress. The Chinese
seemed appalled by the news of the abduction,
the possible involvement of their brethren,
and more so by the possible reprisals that
would fall upon their community.

Clint knew without a doubt a major confrontation could result from the spreading
news of the abductions. Even though the argonauts liked the Californios little more than
they did the Chinese, they seemed to relish
any excuse to fall upon the "yellow infesta-
tion," as the newspaper writers enjoyed la-
beling the Chinatown occupants.

"The chances of finding that girl diminish
drastically as each day passes," Clint groused

to Gideon as they walked back to the El Dorado. "I wish to hell something would turn up."

"Don't give up hope, my friend," Gideon said, laying a hand on Clint's shoulder. "Perseverance and patience pay."

"Unless we turn up some kind of lead, I can't help but think maybe I should be hunting in Sacramento City or the gold country, rather than here."

"Ah, but San Francisco is the obvious first place to look. If the girl was taken inland, you have time to follow. If she's to be transported by ship, then time may be of the essence. You chose correctly."

"I hope so. I have refused the possibility that she may not be alive. For her sake, and her father's, I hope so." They shoved through the batwing doors of the El Dorado.

Luther Baggs set a beer in front of Clint and a flavored soda water in front of Gideon without being asked. He swiped Gideon's money from the bar.

Clint took a deep draw and looked into the mirrors over the backbar, speaking his thoughts aloud. "I gotta figure the Barracoon is involved in the abduction of Apolonia Vega . . . in some way. Still, Zhang Ho was convincing that the Chinese had nothing to do with it."

"It's an evil place," Gideon said quietly. "The skin color is different where I come from, but the purpose is the same. The girl you spoke to seemed cheerful enough. I don't think she understands her fate . . . but I do, too well."

Clint took another deep draw on his beer and wiped the foam away with one of the towels that hung under the bar at six-foot intervals. "True enough. No telling what those women were told in order to get them here. They think they're going to find husbands, or honorable households to work in. I would guess their fates are far worse."

"Knowing men as I do, I agree." Gideon looked around him. His face was expressionless but his eyes spoke of sadness and frustration. He studied the men in the room. "Kindness seems against the nature of man."

"Everything is better in California," Clint said, his tone more hopeful than convinced.

"Men are men, my friend."

"You doubt their ability to change?"

"Have you noticed in your many travels how the good Lord has designed his creatures?" Clint didn't answer. Rather, he waited to see where Gideon was going with this.

"The great cats, the lion, tiger, the wolves, and the raptors . . . eagle, hawk, even the sharks," Gideon continued, a slightly sardonic smile on his face. "All of them have their eyes in the front of their heads. They look forward — the chase is the thing with the predator." Gideon sipped his soda. "The deer, the antelope, the small birds, the little fishes . . . all the creatures preyed upon have their eyes on the sides of their heads. They must watch in all directions. Surviving the predator is the uppermost thing in their lives."

"Is there a point to this?" Clint asked.

"Look around you."

Clint glanced around the room, still not getting Gideon's intent.

"All of them . . . the humans . . . the harbingers of peace on earth, goodwill to men! Those who believe they are made in the very image of God. Eyes in the fronts of their heads, my friend. Predators, each and every one, by their own and God's will. It is their nature." Gideon shook his head in disgust. "As much as it is the nature of the jaguar. Only their fangs and claws are the Colt's, the Bowie, and the lash."

Clint glanced at the people around him — the Chinese, the Peruvian, the Chilean, the Australian, the American. He sipped his beer quietly and thought about Gideon's observation.

Maybe it was the nature of man, even though he was supposedly civilized, to prey

134

on his fellow man.

Clint drank quietly, but his enjoyment was gone. For some reason, the beer tasted bitter.

Yawning, more from frustration than exhaustion, he downed the last of his drink. "I'm going to check on my horse," he said, waving to Gideon and heading for the door.

Outside, he came face-to-face with Don Carlos Vega as he cleared the batwing doors.

"I was told I could find you here," Don Carlos said, a disappointed look on his face.

"Here, Chinatown, the waterfront," Clint said, a little defensively.

"May we talk?" Don Carlos asked.

"Of course." Clint began walking away from the saloon, noticing the five mounted vaqueros who discreetly followed at a distance.

They walked half a block before Don Carlos spoke. "You have had no success?"

"Not enough to speak about yet, Don Carlos. It is very soon. I have met with the Chinese and have talked with the city marshal —"

"And that did no good, I suppose?"

"You were one hundred percent right about the law."

"As I knew." He folded his hands behind his back. "Gaspar Cota and his vaqueros have come to San Francisco to search. He thinks you are a meddling young Anglo fool and that I'm just an old fool."

"I wish him luck. I have no problem with that so long as he doesn't get in my way."

The old don paused before the window of a mercantile. It was filled with all kinds of goods, mostly for the miner. "Ah . . . San Francisco has changed so much. I fear I will never see my daughter again." His eyes looked deep and hollow and his voice wavered.

"I'll find her, if she's in San Francisco."

"Not in some saloon!" the don snapped, his voice suddenly stronger.

"It is a center of information, Don Carlos. You and your men hunt in your way. Let Gaspar hunt in his. I will hunt in mine. If I do not succeed, I do not get paid. I truly hope one of us finds her soon, and I don't care which of us."

"Thank you," Don Carlos said, his voice weak again. He waved at his vaqueros and they spurred their mounts and trotted up, one of them leading the don's horse.

He mounted with an easy swing up into the saddle, belying his age.

"Find my daughter," he said, his voice strong and cold, "and you shall have your horses. If she is not found soon, I fear it will be never."

"If she's in San Francisco, I'll find her," Clint said.

The don nodded, swung his horse, and led

his men away at a gallop.

Clint watched him go. Frustrated when he left the El Dorado, now he felt doubly so. He wished he were truly as sure of his success as he had tried to make Don Carlos Vega believe.

He feared the old don was right.

Soon, or never.

Captain Isaac Banyon stood at the taffrail watching the approaching shore boat being sculled alongside. A single black-clad skull-capped oarsman stood in the rear of the little boat. In her prow reclined Isaac's partner, General Zhang Ho.

"I do not like that Chinaman." Lucretia's voice grated at Isaac from over his shoulder.

"Damn ye, woman, how many times must I tell ye not to slip up on me like that?"

"And how many times must I ask you not to curse, Isaac Banyon?"

Isaac took a deep breath. God, if only he had left his wife behind in Philadelphia. "Get ye below, and ye won't have to deal with the heathen. I like him little more than ye, but business is business."

"It's Satan's business ye do," she muttered, but he could hear her move away to the ladder. He yelled to the cook's helper, Willie Boy Wong, to stand by to assist the general, then strode aft to greet his guest.

Atop the quarterdeck, Stoddard, the first mate, directed two hands to drop a block and tackle line, rigged from a spanker boom with a sling, over to the waiting boat. General Zhang Ho adjusted the sling under his backside while his oarsman held the little boat steady. The men above hauled away, then swung the boom and the general amidships. In a moment, with Willie Boy's help, Zhang Ho stood before the captain, the first mate, and the supercargo, Abner Baggs.

"What brings ye here, General Ho?" Isaac asked. "No problems with the sale, I hope."

"No, Captain. Everything progresses well. There is one small thing, however. . . ." He watched as the captain winced, anticipating more negotiating. "There has been a man named Ryan asking questions regarding the abduction of some Californio women. He and another violated our privacy and the women's quarters at the Barracoon, obviously looking for these women." Ho waited for Banyon's reaction. He got none. "Do you know anything of these abductions?"

Banyon cleared his throat. "Nothing. Is the sale of the women on schedule?"

General Ho refused to be detoured from the matter at hand. "It is very important that we Chinese maintain good relations in this country. We are guests here, as you know, Captain Banyon. We would be very unhappy if anything were to upset our peaceful coexistence. And, of course, our ability to do business. . . . We wouldn't want our partners to suffer along with us." General Ho offered a slight but deferential bow, though his eyes glowed with suspicion.

Banyon perceived Ho's statement as a veiled threat, but did not react. "I understand," he said. "Now, is the auction on schedule? I will not sail until I have my half of the proceeds, plus the cost of the voyage, General. The faster I sail, the faster we will have another load of . . . merchandise to sell."

"We are on schedule. Tomorrow at break of day the buyers will begin inspecting the goods. By nightfall, when they have had plenty of time to admire the quality of the merchandise and to drink enough liquor to loosen their purse strings, the sale will begin."

"Good," Isaac said, and smiled for the first time since General Ho had arrived.

The general bowed slightly and moved back to the rail. Willie Boy helped him into the sling and Ho spoke to him in rapid Chinese. "I want to talk with you. Come to the Barracoon tonight."

"I do not have leave," Willie stammered.

"Come tonight, or join your ancestors," Ho

said, his tone as cold and relentless as a Manchurian winter wind. "My boat will await you at the aft anchor rode at midnight."

"Tonight," Willie quickly agreed, his mouth dry.

They slung Ho up and over the side.

"What did he say?" Captain Banyon asked Willie.

"Nothing, sir," Willie said, not meeting his eyes.

"The hell you say, boy. I have ears."

"He said only to be careful with the sling, sir. If he dropped into the sea, I would meet my ancestors."

Banyon guffawed. He might come to like this General Ho after all. At least he would like him a lot more if the take from the sale of the indenture contracts was large enough to fill another small chest with gold to join those he had hidden in the rudder gear well.

The captain rested a hand on his supercargo's shoulder. "Abner, it's time we took on fresh supplies, replenished the vegetables and chicken and pig pens. If all's well, we'll sail day after tomorrow. I want to go ashore with you. Then we'll stop by the El Dorado so you can bid farewell to your son."

"Aye, Cap'n." Abner's eyes lit up.

"And Stoddard," Banyon continued, "you'll come along. I want to find out who this Ryan is, and why he's interested in our business. Luther Baggs knows more about what's going on in this town than any man I know. I smell a foul wind blowin'."

"Should I bring some men?" Stoddard asked.

"Aye. This Ryan might make a good hand, but it might take a few of us to convince him to sign on. If not him, we still need half a dozen hands."

Stoddard laughed, and even Isaac smiled.

During the long trip from Macao, Su Chin had become the undisputed leader of the more than fifty girls who had been quartered in the cold, damp holds of the *Amnity,* and the go-between with the captain and crew.

The regal status of her bound feet assured her position among the women. Their deference to her and her unusual beauty assured her the attention of the captain and his men.

Su Chin was convinced that the sickness and deprivation of the long trip was taking her to a better life — the violent snowstorm before the blossoming spring.

The daughter of a simple farmer and far-sighted mother who was a forceful woman in her own right — at least in the eyes of her husband — Su Chin had been lucky. Her mother had insisted upon keeping her daughter, not drowning her in the Yangtze, as was the fate of many girl babies, and of binding her feet in the regal manner.

"Su Chin will marry well and bring fortune to our family," her mother had insisted. And she proved to be right . . . at least for a short time. Due to the efforts of a marriage broker who was bribed with her mother's meager savings, Su Chin was selected as the fifth wife of a young but powerful warlord. But shortly after joining her husband's household, the young leader became involved in a territorial dispute and fell victim to the swords of another's warriors. Along with other booty, Su Chin became the sixteenth concubine in a far-off household of women who despised her for her height and beauty and fullness of breast, and did everything they could to make her miserable.

But Su Chin was not one to turn the other cheek. She fought fire with fire and with her clever planting of gossip caused infighting and backbiting among the women — more than had happened in the old lord's court in all the years he had had wives and concubines. When he discovered the root of the continuous bickering and dissension, he immediately ordered her sold.

Captain Isaac Banyon, in the right port at the right time, took one look at her and paid handsomely.

After a fortnight in the hold, Su Chin was given the run of the decks of the *Amnity* and, during the last half of the voyage, the use of the private cabin below the captain and his wife. Su Chin believed she was given this special status because of her bound feet, and the fact that she, of all the girls, could cause little trouble. She had enough trouble just getting around.

She was well into the trip when she discovered the peephole.

After carefully considering her options, and being the clever girl she was, she decided not to stuff a rag into the hole, as was her first impulse, but rather used it, in a most seductive and teasing manner, to display her many charms. By the end of the trip, she knew she had driven Captain Banyon wild.

But no wilder than she intended. Only once in the night had she heard the latch on the door being tried. She had no way of knowing if it was the big, dreadful-looking captain who had been testing for the invitation of an unlocked door. Both the chair under the knob and the latch she had devised discouraged the intruder. The next day, fearing she might have teased too much, she had fetched Willie and, in the presence of the captain's wife, complained about someone trying to enter her quarters.

Later that night she heard the captain's wife screeching in the cabin above.

Her latch never rattled in the night again, though the sound of heavy breathing continued behind the peephole.

Su Chin was happy that the auction was near. She was convinced that she and the other girls would soon be the treasured and revered wives of the white devils — of whom she had come to know and like on the trip.

They were not the eaters of babies that she had been led to believe. They were polite and admiring, and like all men, malleable in the hands of a clever girl.

Su Chin hobbled from room to room along the walkway above the auction floor, talking with the girls.

"Prepare yourselves," she advised. "Brush your hair with a thousand strokes to make it shine like ebony. Stand your tallest and throw your shoulders back so the richness of your womanhood draws the glances of every potential husband or kindly master."

The girls giggled and laughed, most of them now having fully regained their health and vigor.

"Remember to color your cheeks and lips." As soon as she had arrived at the Barracoon, Su Chin had convinced the general to provide them with more blankets and a better variety of food, as well as a few bolts of silk so they could sew properly enticing gowns for those who didn't have anything but peasant clothes. And, as important, abundant face paint — a variety of powders and coloring and scents — as she had convinced him it would greatly increase the return on his investment. Reluctantly, and with some difficulty, he had provided it.

Yes, Su Chin was very happy to be here. It was the beginning of a new life. She hoped the handsome white devil, or his dark friend, surely a rich and respected Javanese or South Pacific islander, would be among the bidders for her contract, or her hand. They were certainly potential bidders, for hadn't they been so anxious to see the China Marys that they had risked the wrath of General Ho's guards to do so?

Either man, or any of a thousand others, would suit her well — if he was rich, and clean, and kind.

CHAPTER
TWELVE

Clint crossed Montgomery Street dodging drays and horsebackers just as the shadows lengthened to envelop it. He entered Mariano's Cold Day Tavern, dragged up a chair, and ordered a beefsteak.

"Rare, and top it with a couple of cackleberries," he instructed the rotund proprietor.

"Cackleberries?" Mariano looked puzzled.

"Eggs, friend." Clint managed a smile, even though frustration gnawed at his gut more than his hunger.

"The only eggs I've seen in a week are duck eggs," the Italian said. "Every farmer is on his way to the gold fields, and they must have taken their hens with them."

"Then whatever you've got." Clint extended his coffee mug, then grimaced as the stream of *brea*-black appeared from the snout of the granite pot Mariano carried. The Italian motioned at a sugar bowl as if it were a requirement for the black syrup, and hurried away. Clint abstained from the sugar, but was pleasantly surprised at the rich flavor of the brew. Mariano's coffee was real, not laced with scorched pinto beans or any of the other fillers that some of the restaurants used.

In moments, Mariano, who also served as cook, bartender, and waiter, returned from the steamy nook that passed for a kitchen. He placed the platter in front of Clint without comment.

After sawing at it with the dull-bladed knife provided by the establishment, Clint drew his own small-bladed skinning knife and carved off a bite of the onion-disguised chunk of rump. *Beef, hell,* he thought. He knew mule when he tasted it — but he had eaten mule before, and at only fifty cents for a meal that included noodles with an Italian name he couldn't pronounce, beans, bread, and coffee, he decided not to complain.

Besides, the bread was hot and fresh out of the oven, and it alone was worth the price of the meal. Though twice the cost of what it had been a year before, the food was still less than most of the eateries in San Francisco.

Clint managed to gnaw the mule into submission, sop up the last of the beans and red sauce with the tender but hard-crusted bread, and was downing the last of his cold coffee when Tok Wu "Huly Up" Hong entered. Since he had sent for him over an hour before, Clint had begun to believe Hong wasn't coming.

Hong pulled up a chair across the rough-hewn table.

"I still have need of information, Huly Up," Clint said, studying the short, wide-shouldered Chinese.

"And Tok Wu have need of money, Mr. Ryan, but have no information about Californio girl for you."

"How about the Barracoon?"

"You not satisfied last night? I understand you foolish enough to break in. It now common knowledge in Chinatown."

"And General Ho?"

"General Ho know everything go on in Chinatown, Mr. Ryan. Some thing he know before Chinatown know."

"Does he know you led us to the Barracoon?"

Hong's head snapped up in alarm. "No, Mr. Ryan, my life not worth duck dung if he find out." He glanced about nervously. "You say nothing?"

"Not a word. What will Ho do if Gideon and I show up at the auction?"

"Nothing. If harmed nothing during your 'visit' to Barracoon, and if bring pouch full money."

"I have no use for a China Mary. I'm only going because I'm interested in the proceedings."

"I think best you bid, even if drop out early."

Clint smiled; then his look turned hard. "You're sure you know of no connection between the Barracoon and General Ho and the missing Californio señoritas?"

"Absolutely not," Hong said with such conviction, and such concise English, Clint believed him.

"Thank you for coming," Clint said as Hong rose to leave.

Damn the flies, Clint thought. *I guess I'll have to go on to Sacramento City and see what I can turn up there. All I'm doin' is suckin' my teeth around here.* Just as Hong reached the door, Clint had another thought. "Huly Up, who else is involved in the Barracoon?"

Hong glanced around, but there was only one other customer in the place, and his head rested on the table next to an empty jug of wine. Mariano was working in the back, banging pots and pans and singing an aria of some seemingly one-note opera. Still, Hong shuffled back to the table before he answered.

"Again, Mr. Ryan, I be killed if General Ho think I talk of Fu Sang Tong business."

Clint reached deep into his pocket reluctantly, dug out another five-dollar gold piece, and placed it on the table.

"Not even to 'sainted mother'?" Hong pressed, darting his eyes around.

Clint nodded and pushed the gold piece across the table.

Hong eyed it nervously, but picked it up. "You are vely persuasive man, Mr. Ryan. General Ho's partner white devil." He looked slightly embarrassed at using the term, but Clint merely nodded his encouragement. "The captain of *Amnity*, ship that brought China Marys across Pacific, said to be honorable partner."

"Thank you, Huly Up. That is interesting news."

Hong hurried to the door and was gone. Wanting to shout a hooray, Clint instead left a generous tip for the Italian — even if the beefsteak was mule.

"Hurry up, Willie Boy," Abner Baggs chided the Chinese cook's helper as they descended the ladder to the rooms below the captain's cabin. Abner set his bowls down on the floor and fumbled with his keys, while Willie balanced two of the hot receptacles on each arm. Abner had enlisted Willie's help so he would not have to make two trips.

"Now, Willie, like I told you, don't be saying nothing to no one about these here señoritas. If'n I wasn't in such a hurry to go ashore with the captain, I wouldn't be lettin' you see."

"Happy help, Mista Baggs, sir."

"If'n we weren't sailing day after tomorrow, I wouldn't dare let you in on this. But the cap'n says we'll be out with the tide then."

Abner gave the boy his sternest eye, and Willie grinned widely, nodding until his short queue bobbed.

Abner swung the door aside and led Willie Boy in. The women were each in their respective bunks. Abner set the bowls of gruel, each with a wooden spoon, chunk of salt pork, and dollop of molasses, on the deck, and Willie Boy followed suit. The Chinese boy stared wide-eyed from bunk to bunk, saying nothing.

Señora Juanita Robles swung her legs out of the low bunk and rose, her voice shaking. "Señor Baggs, surely it is not that loathsome gruel again."

"Don't be complainin', Señorita!" Abner scowled.

"It is Señora, Mr. Baggs, not Señorita. I am a married woman, one who wants to return to her husband!" This elicited no response out

151

of the old man. "We are out of candles again, and the chamber pots are in need of emptying. We must launder these terrible smocks, and we need more towels."

"It'll be morning afore we get to any of it."

"But we must have candles —"

Ignoring her requests, Abner pushed Willie out the door in front of him.

"And the chamber pots!" Juanita Robles yelled, and began to beat on the door. Apolonia rose and hurried to her. Tears were pouring out of Juanita's eyes and she was trembling uncontrollably.

"Why are they keeping us here?" Juanita sobbed, finally breaking down after a week's imprisonment on gruel, salt pork, molasses, and water.

Apolonia held her until she quieted, then looked her directly in the eye. "Now, do you see the futility in waiting? We *must* escape. No one has come to our aid, and no one will, for they do not know where we are. It is up to us. Only us."

Juanita, who until this instant had been so strong, looked hopeless. Then her tears stopped and her eyes steeled. She lifted her chin, but her hands still trembled. "As you say, it is up to us."

The other girls rose and hurried to join them, a group now united by a common purpose. Each looked at the other, awaiting a plan. Awaiting a leader.

A week ago she would not have had the courage, but now Apolonia decided she had no choice.

Clint walked to the waterfront and stood on the wharf. With the help of a dockworker, he picked out the packet ship *Amnity,* moored a little over two cable lengths out in the harbor. She lay quiet, with little activity on deck. Her anchor lantern was lit, but few other lights glowed through her ports. Convinced by the inactivity that she was not sailing tonight nor on the morning's tide, he returned to the El Dorado.

Having retired to the room he had rented for some much-needed sleep, Gideon was nowhere in sight. Clint bulled his way to the bar and ordered a beer. The saloon was its usual rowdy din, but, as usual, quieted when Sultry took the stage.

By the time she had finished her third song and the bald-headed pianoforte player had begun gathering the coins and nuggets from the stage floor, Clint felt a tap on his shoulder.

"Ye be Clint Ryan?" Clint turned to face a man of equal height, but thicker than Clint, with a full gray beard spread across his chest.

Clint hesitated a moment, for he was still

153

a wanted man for his "malfeasance" aboard ship, and this man was clearly an officer of the sea even though he carried no braid or insignia on his well-tailored black suit. But if the man sought him for the problems of the *Savannah,* he would hardly tap him on the shoulder.

"Yes, I'm Clint Ryan."

The man extended his hand in a businesslike manner, and Clint shook as Captain Isaac Banyon introduced himself. Clint, slightly taken aback, held his tongue. This was the man who captained the only ship in a harbor of eight hundred that Clint wanted to board.

"Can I buy you a drink, Captain?" Clint offered, signaling the bartender for another mug of Dog's Head ale.

"Demon rum is the devil's own, Mr. Ryan. I will partake of a glass of clean water, or cool cow's or goat's milk, if available."

Luther Baggs delivered Captain Banyon a glass of water without argument, then took up a friendly animated conversation with the man who accompanied the captain.

"How is it you know me, Captain Banyon?" Clint asked, carefully sipping his beer.

"I make it my business to know every able-bodied man in the harbors I visit, Mr. Ryan, and you look able-bodied enough. We need hands, sir. We sail on the tide, day after tomorrow. Would ye be interested in signing aboard the finest packet ship in the Pacific?"

It must be quite a task to know every able-bodied man among more than twenty thousand, Clint thought, wondering what was the true reason the captain had sought him out. "What cargo are you hauling, Captain?"

"The usual, lumber and iron to China, silk and china and fancy doodads to tempt the ladies of New England in return." Banyon cut his eyes away, a dead giveaway for a lie, Clint surmised.

"I'm currently employed, Captain Banyon. Otherwise I'd be proud to serve on a fine ship. I spent many years at sea and, if I may say so, I am a skilled mariner."

"As I suspected, Mr. Ryan. I can always spot a man of the sea." The big captain made an attempt at a smile, then took a drink of his water. He backhanded drops from his beard. "That is unfortunate, for the *Amnity* not only is a fine ship, but she's a friendship — a percent of the voyage's profits fall to even the common sailor." Banyon's eyes narrowed. "And, if I may ask, what is your current employment, Mr. Ryan?"

Caution waved a flag and Clint hesitated before answering. There was no sense in alarming a man he had already perceived as an enemy. "I've taken a job as a guide for the one and only Sultana Mulvany."

"You'd work for a woman?" The captain's bushy eyebrows narrowed until they touched.

"Not merely a woman, Captain. The most beautiful woman ever to bless the stage — hell, maybe the country. And she needs a guide."

"Well, if that be ye choice." The captain turned his back on Clint. "We be on our way, Abner Baggs. Say your good-byes to Luther."

Clint watched as the older man shook with the bulldog bartender. Luther Baggs knew exactly what Clint was about, and he was obviously related to a sailor on the *Amnity*.

This should teach you to keep the slack out of your tongue, Clint chided himself, knowing that everything Luther Baggs had overheard him say had been told to the *Amnity*. And the *Amnity* crew and her captain were now far too interested in what Clint was up to.

And if the captain had sought him out, then the captain must have something to hide. He wanted to be on board the *Amnity*, but he would be damned if he would do so by signing aboard. No, there had to be another way to get on board the ship, and now that he knew when she planned to sail, he knew just how to go about it.

Clint studied the broad-shouldered captain as he left, noticing that five other men, obviously sailors, from their duck pants and striped shirts, followed. One man, particularly big and sporting a soup-strainer mustache, locked gazes with Clint until he passed through the door. The captain had come in force.

Maybe for a last drink for the crew . . . or maybe for something else?

Clint wondered if he was that something else.

CHAPTER THIRTEEN

Clint sipped his beer slowly and glanced at Luther Baggs out of the corner of his eye. The potato-faced bartender moved up and down the bar, wiping with a wet cloth, picking up mugs and glasses. Finally Clint waved him over.

"You related to the man with Captain Banyon?"

"My pa. The supercargo of a full-rigged packet ship and the best at his trade." Baggs swiped at the polished planks with a towel.

"And he's off again to the Orient?"

"Aye. Day after tomorrow."

"Did you come here on the *Amnity?*"

"As a working passenger. She brought a load of argonauts on her last voyage from Philadelphia, like every other vessel from the East."

"And she seeks more crew?"

Baggs stopped and looked up from his work.

"Are you writing a journal, Clint Ryan?"

Clint flashed a knife-edged smile. "No, but I find it a bit strange that the captain sought me out. Did you mention me to him?"

Baggs went back to his wiping. "I tell my father of any able-bodied man who might be tempted to sign on. I may have mentioned you."

"What cargo has your father been gathering for the crossing?"

Baggs turned his back on Clint and began shining glasses. "The usual — iron, tools, manufactured goods . . . though it's difficult, as all the goods in San Francisco are in demand."

"I'd like to speak with your pa, Luther. Could you arrange it? I might be able to help him locate some cargo." Clint paused. "No one knows California better than I."

Luther turned from his work. A slow smile crept across his face. "My pa is always anxious to find another agent who'd bring him some cargo. I could arrange a meeting this very night if you think you might help him . . . and yourse'f, a'course."

"Then do it." Clint managed a smile, but feared it was as hollow as the one returned by the bartender.

"Don't go away."

Clint nodded and tipped up his mug.

Luther chuckled to himself as he made his way down the long bar. His father had instructed him to pour generous drinks for Clint Ryan. Stoddard and Captain Banyon had plans for him, so Luther had laced the last two beers with a shot of powerful rum. But this would be better and faster, for the fool had actually asked to meet with his pa.

After finding his way through the storage room to the side door of the saloon, Luther pulled it open and checked up and down the dark alley before he ventured out. The fog had begun to crawl into the city. Even the areas normally lit by the upstairs windows of the El Dorado lay hidden. It wouldn't do for him to be shanghaied by another ship's crew or any of the roving bands who found an easy living performing that function. He was supposed to be helping his father fill the crew of the *Amnity*.

Quickly Luther worked his way along the narrow cleft between the two-story buildings to the alley entrance, where he could see the silhouette of several lingering men.

"Stoddard!" Luther called out to the distinctive broad-shouldered image that loomed near the alley opening.

The massive form rolled away from the wall and settled into an arms-at-the-ready, legs-spread stance and his mates arranged them-

selves behind him as Luther approached —
happy that he wasn't the man they truly
awaited.

"Where's my pa?" Luther demanded.

Stoddard recognized him, then looked disappointed that he was not a prospect. "He's
off with the captain. They said for us to wait
here, just in case Ryan left the saloon afore
they returned."

"Well —" Luther managed a chuckle, "the
fool's asked to meet with Pa. Send a man to
fetch him. Pa will talk with him outside, then
you can knot his noggin and tote him away."

"I don't know where they be," Stoddard
said, scratching his lip under the thick mustache. "But it's no matter. Tell Ryan your
father waits in the alley."

"He's not fool enough to wander into a dark
alley. And I hear tell that he's handy with
that Colt's rifle and handgun. You best send
for Pa and the captain."

Stoddard's shoulders hulked and his chin
thrust forward. Even as alleywise and handy
with his fists as Baggs was, he slinked before
the powerful first mate. "I said tell Ryan your
father waits in the alley. Do it."

Baggs nodded quickly and worked his way
back down the mist-occluded alley to the bar's
rear door. He paused before entering the
safety of the saloon and called back.

"I'll tell'm, but don't blame me if he don't come." Baggs disappeared into the El Dorado's alley door.

As Luther made his way through the storeroom and opened the door to the smoky saloon full of shouting and laughing men, his gut relaxed. He moved down the bar, convinced that he knew a way to get Ryan into the alley and to keep his pa out of it. Though a common practice, shanghaiing was against one of the many new city ordinances in San Francisco.

He waved Ryan over to the bar, and the man bulled his way through the crowd.

"I couldn't find my pa, but your Ethiopian friend . . . Gideon LaMont . . ."

Clint riveted his attention on the bartender.

"He's out in the alley. Seems his big black ass has finally had a little too much to drink. You better see to him afore the shanghaiers find the easy pickin's."

Clint brought his ever-present Colt's rifle up, spun on his heel, and used its muzzle to get through the crowd. The men parted easily as the rifle's cold threat worked its steely way between them.

Gideon had been sober and on his way to his room, Clint remembered as he made his way out of the El Dorado. This smelled as fishy as the hold of the cod-bank schooner Clint had worked on when he first went to sea.

Clint paused on the boardwalk in the light of one of the El Dorado's tall windows, checked the loads in his Colt's rifle and re-volving breech pistol, then moved to the open-ing of the alley.

No one was in sight down its dark length — but half a dozen eight-hundred-pound grizzlies could easily be waiting among the many crates and barrels and deep-shadowed doorways.

He surveyed the street, which was quieter than earlier but still far from vacant. Figures moved in and out of the patchy fog and a few wagons still plodded along. Then he turned to the alley. It felt like worms gnawed at his vitals and his eyes, cold and gray as the night fog, darted at every hiding place. His calloused thumb found the iron hammer of the rifle. Pausing, he allowed his eyes to adjust to the dank darkness. Then he started forward.

The gravel alley crunched underfoot. Lights from windows on the second story of the El Dorado cast deep shadows near the middle of the pathway, and the street at the far end was only slightly less black than the alley itself. Clint stiffened, hearing a scratching sound. He put it off as the scurrying of a rat.

He caught a movement out of the corner of his eye and a swinging piece of lumber flashed out of the shadows, crashing into the barrel of his rifle. Clint swung the heavy muzzle upward, slamming it under his attacker's chin. The man's head snapped backward and Clint caught the flash of the whites of his eyes.

Then powerful arms enveloped him and a blow racked the side of his head.

Clint dropped to his knees and rolled out of the grasp of the man, kicking his legs out from under him. The man crashed heavily to the gravel with an *oooff*.

A club slammed into Clint's shoulder and he felt his Colt's rifle being wrenched away by another attacker who had climbed out of the pile of barrels and boxes.

Instinctively Clint scrambled to get his back to the wall. At the same time he pawed for his Colt's revolver — and found the holster empty.

He tensed for the next attack as the four men left standing formed up in front of him.

Sultry Mulvany sat at her dressing table, redoing her makeup. She heard the muffled sounds of blows and the clatter of boxes in the alley below her window. Against her better judgment she rose and walked to the tall narrow glass and peered down at the dark shadowy alley below.

One man lay unmoving, sprawled in the alley, and four burly men surrounded another with his back to the wall. The men held clubs and Sultry caught the reflection of light from a gun barrel. The man with his back to the wall kicked out and caught one of his attackers in the belly as he charged, driving back and doubling the man, but another swung his bludgeon and drove the attacked man to his knees, knocking his hat flying. Sultry caught a flash of color and recognized the sandy hair.

She ran to the door and shouted down the stairs.

Jasper Henry was relaxing in a chair near the stage door, his feet propped up, his slouch hat covering his bald head and pulled low over his eyes. He almost fell from his roost at the high-pitched urgency of her voice.

"Help that man in the alley!"

He stepped to the curtain and yelled to the six burly bartenders before venturing out the stage door. Thinking that Sultry had a problem, they came at a run.

Clint's head swam and one arm and leg were pinned by two sailors, but still he pummeled with his free fist. He could taste the blood in his mouth and feel the hot rush that poured over his face from a gash in his head.

His head crashed against a brick wall, crushed between the heavy men and the bricks. He clawed, momentarily cheered as he felt his thumb plunge deep into an eye socket, but then a club flashed and again his head snapped backward. Blows rained over him, so many they were indistinguishable.

Clint fought to retain consciousness, but reeled deeper and deeper into blackness. He couldn't feel or hear the club as it smacked into flesh and crunched into bone.

The fog enveloped him, and with it a vision of a terrible storm he had fought at Tierra del Fuego. He was hanging in the ice-covered shrouds, his hands frozen, unable to move.

CHAPTER
FOURTEEN

Willie Boy Wong swung his legs out of his bunk in the fo'c'sle and padded to the ladder, carrying his low-heeled leather boots so as not to disturb the other sleeping crewmen. He mounted the ladder and paused on the holystoned pine deck to pull on the boots as he scanned the dark decks of the *Amnity* for signs of the anchor watch. Marvin Vandersteldt, the second mate, stood at the wheel on the aft quarterdeck. Willie could see the flare of his cigar. He knew Marvin would be armed to the teeth and instructed to shoot to kill any man attempting to jump ship.

With the deckhouse concealing him from Vandersteldt, Willie crept forward. He was in a terrible quandary. The anchor watch stood near the wheel, on the aft of the ship, and General Ho had said his boat would wait at the aft anchor rode. It would be very difficult — impossible — for Willie to climb down the aft anchor rode without being seen by the watch.

Unless he could entice the man forward or below decks.

As he neared the forward ladder, he heard a quiet pounding from deep in the bowels of the ship. He craned his neck so he could make out the man at the wheel, and wondered if he, too, could hear the noise from below — but Marvin made no move. Willie descended the half ladder to the deck accommodating the captain's cabin and officers' mess, then descended the full ladder below to the passengers' quarters, where he knew the women were kept.

The pounding was coming from inside the women's door. He paused and leaned close. "What ladies want?"

Apolonia stopped pounding, her hold growing tight on the chamber pot she held. This could be their chance. "Get ready," she commanded in a harsh whisper to the others. "Someone is here."

She leaned close to the door. "Please, Señor. Señora Robles is very ill. Open the door."

Juanita Robles took her place on the deck in the center of the cabin, held her stomach with both hands, and began to moan softly. The other girls assumed their places on either

168

side of the door. A teak stanchion, worked carefully from one of the bunks by the combined efforts of all of them, and Apolonia's chamber pot, would serve as clubs.

"What kind sick?" Willie asked through the door.

"I don't know, but she needs a *médico*."

Apolonia leaned hopefully against the jamb, silently praying that the man outside would open the lock and offer them their chance. Then she heard his footfalls padding away. Crestfallen, she turned to the others. "He's leaving."

They made their way back to their bunks, and Juanita Robles rose from the floor. As Apolonia sank into her narrow cubicle, she heard the quiet sobs of one of the girls. It only steeled her resolve.

She had hardly settled into her narrow berth when she heard the footfalls of someone returning, the clinking of a key in the lock, and the tumblers being turned. With a rush, the women returned to their places.

Willie Boy Wong stepped into the dark room, and Apolonia brought the crockery chamber pot across his head. Shards scattered over the room. The little Chinese collapsed to the deck beside the feigning Juanita as if his legs were chopped off at the knees.

"What the devil!" Marvin Vandersteldt

169

charged into the doorway and grabbed Apolonia's wrist, wrenching the remains of the pot away.

Apolonia screamed in pain, and Juanita lurched forward, wrapping her arms around Marvin's legs and sinking her teeth deeply into his calf.

He yelled and kicked her loose, but the stanchion flashed out of the darkness and caught him flush on the forehead, tumbling him into a black corner of the room.

"Run, girls, run!" Juanita yelled, stepping over Willie Boy on her way out. She dashed for the ladder, with Apolonia and the others close behind, shouting their encouragement.

As they topped the ladder, Lucretia Banyon opened her own cabin door and, Bible in hand, watched them ascend the half ladder to the main deck.

"May God have mercy on your soul, Isaac Banyon," Lucretia murmured, hugging the Bible to her chest. She closed and locked the captain's cabin door and returned to her rocking chair.

The women, smocked and barefoot, gathered together on the deck, clinging to one another for reassurance.

The *Amnity* lay in the quiet of high tide, her furled topgallants obscured by the night fog. Cold enveloped Apolonia, and her bones suddenly felt like spikes of ice. She shivered uncontrollably. The lights of the city in the distance came and went like distant fireflies behind gray gauze curtains.

"We must find a boat!" Apolonia whispered harshly, forcing her shaking to stop and breaking the clasp of fear that bound the women to silence. She climbed up on the quarterdeck and spotted the small six-man captain's boat in its davits.

"Here!" she called, motioning to the others, who gathered at the ladder to join her. They began to claw at the lines at each davit, pulling and tugging to release the boat — but the strength of the sailors' routine knots was too much for them.

Apolonia pushed the others aside and began to work on the knot binding the aft line, carefully studying it as she pulled on this end, then that, then at a tuck in the knot. Juanita worked on the bow.

"It's coming!" Juanita cried out.

"Mine too." Apolonia's voice shook with the glimmer of hope, real hope, for the first time.

Juanita's attempts were successful a split second before Apolonia's and the bow of the little boat began to fall toward the black sea below.

"Oh, no!" Juanita cried, as Apolonia's side

began to drop. Apolonia and Juanita both grasped for the lines, but Juanita's had begun to run and it jerked her hands upward into the block, tearing the flesh from her palm. She yelped in pain and jerked away, closing her eyes and bringing her bleeding hand to her mouth. But Apolonia was successful in bringing her end to a halt — which was exactly the wrong thing to do.

The bow dropped and the full weight of the vessel came to bear on the aft line, jerking the rope from Apolonia's hand. With the whine of free-falling hemp and spinning blocks, the little boat plunged bow first into the sea. The women stared in horror as their hopes of escape floundered below, then floated to the surface filled to the gunwales with water.

"Who goes there?" The shout rang out of the fog. The longboat, with the captain, first mate, supercargo, and four crew members appeared out of the fog, followed by another longboat full to her gunwales with trussed men. "Belay that, ye papist wench," Isaac Banyon yelled, and the oarsmen pulled with added vigor to bring the longboat alongside.

"Run! Hide!" Apolonia cried in desperation, and plunged for the ladder to the main deck. She reached it just as Marvin Vandersteldt topped the rail and grabbed for her, ripping the front of her smock away.

"No!" she yelled, fighting for her modesty. The other women ran in every direction. Willie Boy Wong topped the ladder behind Vandersteldt, who shoved Apolonia into Willie's arms and ran in pursuit of another of the fleeing women.

Banyon and the longboat reached the ship, and men began climbing up the rope ladder left hanging for their return.

Willie Boy held tightly to one of Apolonia's arms and watched Vandersteldt chase one of the women across the deck while the others searched for recesses and shadows in which to hide. Seeing his distraction, Apolonia raked the nails of her free hand across his face.

He screamed and shoved her away. She ran for the rail, stared into the blackness, and cursed herself for not knowing how to swim. Frantically she looked for a hiding place. She scampered down the ladder to the main deck and ran forward just as the yellow-toothed first mate leaped over the rail. Fear flooded her. She tried to stop but panicked. Her feet became tangled and she tumbled head over heels to the deck. Stoddard reached down and jerked her to her feet, spinning her around and holding both her arms behind her. She tried to kick backward at him, but he pulled her close and his powerful calloused fingers dug deeply into her arms. The pain stopped her cold.

"Now, Polly," he said, bending his head over her shoulder, close enough that his mustache tickled her cheek and she recoiled at his rancid breath. "Don't ye be makin' it harder on ye'sef than already 'tis."

Captain Isaac Banyon reached the taffrail and leapt over it to face her. Seeing his bulging stare, she realized that her smock hung open.

Her face flushed crimson. "Please, let me cover myself," she pleaded.

"You have no rights aboard this vessel," Banyon spat, but his eyes would not meet hers. His were fixed on the sight of the helpless woman in front of him, and what her torn smock revealed.

"Let that girl go, you evil men." The sound of Lucretia's voice rang with righteous indignation across the deck.

The captain instructed Stoddard to release her, but he already had. Apolonia sank to her knees and pulled her smock closed, holding it in front of her with both hands, her head bowed, fighting to keep the tears from falling in front of her captors.

All over the deck, surprised men chased the other women.

The women were collected, kicking and

screaming curses in Spanish, and were dragged below.

But Lucretia Banyon crossed the deck and protectively cradled the kneeling Apolonia's head against her skirt. She could feel the child sobbing, but the girl kept it quietly to herself.

The crew dropped a line overboard from the aft spanker boom and began loading the trussed bundles from the second longboat.

"Come on, child. I'll take you below and mend the rips in your smock."

Apolonia climbed to her feet wearily, and meekly followed Lucretia Banyon to the rear ladder. She stopped just before she reached it and looked back, wide-eyed, with a combination of hope and disbelief.

The load the sailors hoisted was the bundled, slightly rotund Gaspar Cota. He was gagged, but his eyes glared wild as a caged cougar. The sailors swung him over the taffrail and he caught Apolonia's gaze for a fleeting second while spinning on the end of the mizzen halyard.

"Get ye below!" Banyon's voice startled her, and his rough hand shoved her along to the ladder.

No longer able to see her betrothed, but for the first time *pleased* to see him, she quickly followed Lucretia Banyon into the captain's cabin.

Before anyone returned to the anchor watch, Willie Boy Wong, dead aft behind the wheel, looked down into the murky blackness, searching for General Ho's boat. A trickle of blood found its way out of Willie's hairline, where the girl's chamber pot had found its mark, and lined his cheek.

"Dive in the water." A voice, speaking Chinese in a harsh whisper, rose from the deep shadow of the hull.

"I cannot swim," Willie answered, his voice an octave higher than usual.

"I said dive in," the voice repeated.

Willie glanced over his shoulder, making sure no one watched, stepped to the top of the rail, held his nose with one hand and his aching forehead with the other hand, looked upward and silently advised his ancestors that he was sure to be with them soon, then leapt out into the darkness.

Clint tried to roll over as he awoke, but firm hands restrained him. He lashed out.

"Whoa there, Ryan!" Jasper Henry stepped out of Clint's reach. Clint's eyes finally converted the blurs to recognizable figures, and he was glad they did, for Sultry Mulvany, an image of beauty except for the bloody wet rag in her hand, stood near Jasper Henry.

The room was small, but papered from an

oak chair rail to the ceiling, and carpeted expensively. A crystal chandelier hung from the ceiling and refracted light in dancing rainbow spots on the room's rose-colored walls. A dressing table with graceful Queen Anne legs and loaded with small bottles, jars, and tortoiseshell brushes and combs rested under a large mirror lined with polished silver whale-oil lamps. The settee and three cherry-wood straight-backed chairs with brocaded green fabric seats finished off the feminine decor. The door stood ajar, and Clint made out Sultana Mulvany's name in gold letters.

"The battle's over, Mr. Ryan," she said. She stepped forward and lightly sat on the edge of the settee he rested on. "Let me get the rest of your face cleaned up."

"Who won?" he asked, trying to smile, but his mouth would not quite function.

"Looked like a draw to me," Sultry said. "At least until Jasper and the boys got there. Then the riffraff decided on a strategic retreat and carried off their wounded."

"You was a cooked goose when we got there, and they was ready to spit out the bones," Jasper said.

"There were two down and three to go." Sultry smiled and laid a soft reassuring hand on his arm. "Given the odds, I'd say you did real well."

"I thought you could hit a bluetail fly on the wing with that Colt," Jasper chided.

This time Clint managed a smile. "That was a green horsefly, Jasper . . . and these bugs got behind me. Thanks for the help. I owe you a bottle of Noble's Finest."

"Humph," he grumbled.

Sultry leaned down and her blond hair cascaded over her shoulder, covering half the swell of her breasts, where Clint's eyes seemed to stray. The stage dress was red satin trimmed with black lace and wide with petticoats. Clint caught the delicate odor of lilac water as her gentle touch worked at a cut in his hairline.

It was almost worth the beating.

Lying back, he relaxed as best he could, every movement an exercise in which joint or bruise hurt the most. But his limbs seemed to be functioning. At least nothing was broken. And his eyes worked fine. He tried to keep them on hers, but they kept falling to a tiny heart-shaped mole on the inner cleft of her ample left breast.

"That should have a stitch or at least some plaster," Sultry told him with concern, dabbing at his head.

"I'll heal without." Clint's gaze found her eyes and he got a smile for his trouble. Sultry rose, wadded up the rag, and tossed it to Jasper Henry. She returned to her dressing table.

Clint suddenly realized he didn't have the Colts. "My guns?"

"They're under the settee." Jasper motioned. "Those boys was lucky to get away with their hides."

Just as Clint remembered why he had been in the alley in the first place, Gideon LaMont rapped on the open door to Sultry's dressing room with the gold handle of his walking stick.

"Come in, Mr. LaMont," Sultry said, seeing his image in her mirror. Gideon snatched the high hat off his head and entered.

He took in his beaten and reclining friend with a sweep of his dark eyes. "I understand you took on half the crew of the *Amnity*." Gideon crossed the room, his lips curling in a smile but his eyes reflecting his worry.

"The *Amnity?*" The vision of the granite-shouldered, mustached man that Clint had locked eyes with as Banyon left the El Dorado flashed into his mind and came together with the man he had seen in the alley.

Clint tried to rise, then decided to wait awhile before attempting the maneuver.

"The *Amnity*," Gideon repeated. "One of the bartenders knew half those boys in the alley. Seems they're a bit short of crew and must have thought you'd make a hand."

"That son of a bitch." Clint swung his booted feet to the floor. Sultry glanced back at him from her dresser. "I'm sorry, Miss Mulvany. It's that bartender of yours. Baggs. He told me Gideon was in the alley, liquored up and near passed out. I went looking for him and found the crew of his father's ship."

"Don't blame Baggs on me, Mr. Ryan. Luther Baggs works for the El Dorado, just as I do."

Clint struggled to his feet. "I need to have a chat with Luther."

Sultry crossed the room and placed her hands softly on his shoulders, pushing him gently but firmly back on the settee. Clint winced, but sank back down willingly.

"That'll wait until tomorrow or the next day. You need to rest. I've got two more shows. Then I'll fetch you some soup."

Jasper Henry's jaw tightened and he frowned, but he said nothing.

Sultry returned to her mirror and talked as she applied some color to her cheeks. "You can sleep right there on the settee."

"Sultry —" Jasper growled.

"Right there on the settee, and I'll get you some soup after my last appearance. By then I'll be ready for something to eat myself." She rose and her red satin skirts reflected the light from the whale-oil lamps as she moved to the door. "Don't you go away, Mr. Ryan. Come on, Jasper." She nodded politely to Gideon and was gone in a whirl of petticoats, with Jasper hulking along behind, scratching his gleaming bald head and scowling.

Clint looked at Gideon, feeling a little bit foolish. "He said you were drunk and lying out in the alley."

"That happened when I was twelve. My friend and I snuck some of the LaMonts' rum." Gideon pulled one of the straight-backed chairs over and sat astride it. "My head hurt for a week and my backside for a month . . . after my daddy got through whippin' on it. We were lucky it was daddy who found us, for the LaMonts might have done a lot worse. Liquor is a horsewhippin' offense for a slave. And though a freedman, I don't think it wise for me to be uninhibited by the effects of the demon rum. It's hard enough for a body to get along in this world. I appreciate the worry, but don't fall for that again."

"I'm damn lucky to be here to get that lecture."

"I agree."

The raucous sounds of the saloon quieted, the piano tinkled, and they heard Sultry begin the strains of "Greensleeves."

Gideon rose and returned his hat to his head. "Lucky to be here — and extra lucky to have the self-appointed nurse you do. I'm going back to the saloon to admire her, then to the faro table. I won't be far. I think that beautiful lady has taken a real shine to you. You rest."

"A shine? Don't count on that. I've never had much of a way with the ladies."

"And I've found that it's the ladies who let us know if we have a way with them or not. If they take a shine to you, you got a way. If not, you've lost your way. You rest."

"Yes, sir." Clint had his eyes closed by the time Gideon reached the door.

Gideon hesitated in the doorway, his voice rumbling low. "Clint . . . thanks for worryin' about me."

Clint said nothing. As far as Gideon knew, he was already asleep.

CHAPTER FIFTEEN

General Zhang Ho, resplendent in a black robe with a yellow bird of paradise embroidered on it, reclined in a pillow-lined, carved mahogany chair, his slender well-manicured hands draped casually over the dragon heads that graced the arms. He splayed his fingers through his black hair, smoothing the slash of white that highlighted it on one side, and studied the shivering figure who knelt on the floor in front of him. Two thick-chested, full-bellied guards flanked him, paying little heed to the water-soaked rat of a man who awaited his questions.

Ho slowly stroked each foot-long tail of his dangling mustache, then stepped forward and motioned to one of the guards. "Bring him some tea and a robe."

Willie Boy nodded a thank you and managed a wan smile.

"Rise and take a seat, Wong," Ho instructed, and Willie hurried to one of three smaller chairs that faced Ho's. He did not sit down, but stood beside it, awaiting the general's return to his own seat. The general fluffed his pillows before he sat, then reclined into them. Willie sat rigidly on the edge of his straight-backed chair.

"I have come as you ordered, honorable Ho."

"You have come even though the white devils you work for would not approve. You are a wise young man. In fact, wise beyond your years, and I wish you a long life . . . that is, if you will truthfully answer a few questions."

"My truths are no more a test of my obedience than my coming here, honorable Ho. Did I not jump into the cold dragon-filled waters of the hostile sea at the order of the Fu Sang Tong?"

Ho stifled a smile at the eloquence of this young man, even though the quiet bay was far from a "hostile sea."

"Then tell me, what cargo does the captain who brought the *mui gai* here plan to carry on his return?"

"There is much pig iron in the holds, and also iron tools."

"And?"

"That is all I have seen."

"And passengers?"

"There are women, but I do not understand their position. They are kept under lock and key, and not treated as passengers."

"Chinese women?"

"No, honorable Ho, Californio women."

Zhang Ho stroked his long mustache. It was as he suspected. The captain had assembled a cargo of women for the return trip, probably to sell to the same brokers and warlords who provided the *mui gai*. To Ho, Californio girls were large and clumsy, but they seemed beautiful in their cowlike way, and they would be an oddity in the courts of China. Yes, they would bring a high price — a price Captain Banyon had no intention of sharing with his partner. A price, and a cargo, that would reflect badly on all Celestials in the *gum san*.

Zhang Ho understood that the Celestials had already been blamed for the abductions, for were the abductors not dressed as Chinese? Yes, perhaps Captain Isaac Banyon was also a student of Sun Tzu and the ancient art of war. Divide and confuse the enemy. But not a good enough student, for Sun Tzu did not teach doing so at the expense of valued friends.

It was imperative, even as valuable as Captain Isaac Banyon and the *Amnity* were to the tong, that he not be allowed to bring the wrath of the white devils down upon the Celestials.

Ho returned his attention to Willie. "When does the captain plan to sail?"

"I have been told that we sail day after tomorrow."

But not without his money, Zhang Ho knew. *Not without his half of the proceeds from the sale of the* mui gai *contracts. No, he will not sail until I pay. That will give me time to make sure the Californio women are released.*

The best of all possible solutions would be to have Captain Banyon believe someone else caused their escape, so the tong could retain his goodwill and the use of his ship. But at all costs they must be set free.

Zhang rose as one of the *mui gai,* whose services he had decided to use until the sale, returned with the tea. "My men will return you to the ship after you've finished your tea," he told Willie. "Do not be caught climbing back on board. Tell no one of your visit with me. I will call upon you again before you sail and your help will not be forgotten by the Fu Sang."

"Thank you, General Ho," Willie said, jumping to his feet as the general rose. "I will await your summons . . . and possibly, someday, Willie Wong might enjoy the comradeship of the Fu Sang as a member."

"Possibly," Ho said.

Zhang left the meeting room for his private quarters to reflect upon what he'd learned. But he knew one thing for sure: the white devil, Clint Ryan, who came to him seeking news of the Californio girls, could be the solution to his problem.

Clint awoke to the odor of beef stew and freshly baked bread. Sultry had her back to him dishing up the stew from a crock on her dressing table. She'd changed out of her red satin stage dress into a black silk wrapper. The whale-oil lamps surrounding her mirror showed off the soft curves of her body and highlighted her long blond hair. The pattern of her black silk stockings showed beneath her flimsy wrap, and her trim ankles and small feet were bare except for the fancy stockings.

She must have sensed his eyes on her.

"I've got coffee or wine," she said without turning.

"Wine now, coffee later."

She turned and brought him a bowl and spoon. The V in her wrapper showed enough cleavage that his favorite mole was exposed, and below it, a red silk flower on the tightly fitting corset that thrust her breasts up and sucked her waist into two hand-spans. She set the soup down and went back to fill a mug with rich red wine from a carafe.

Clint took a mouthful of the stew and realized how hungry he was. Sultry handed him a mug and seated herself. She held her glass out and toasted him, her countenance serious but her blue eyes laughing.

"Here's to not taking any unplanned ocean voyages."

"I'll drink to that."

They drank, and Clint studied her carefully as she picked at her food. "You've been awfully kind to a stranger, ma'am."

"Not a stranger. We were properly introduced by my friend Jasper Henry."

"Friend?"

"Yes, Mr. Ryan. Friend. Jasper is my employee and traveling companion."

"Nothing else?"

She watched him a moment. Then she smiled softly. "If you're going to ask such forward questions, Mr. Ryan, perhaps we should be on a first-name basis. My friends call me Sultry."

"Sultry. Clint, please. Jasper didn't seem too happy that you allowed me to rest here."

"He's neither father, brother, nor chaperon, Clint. I'm my own woman."

"That you are, ma'am — and all woman at that, if you don't mind me saying so."

Sultry took a sip of her wine, but her eyes never left Clint's. She dabbed at her mouth.

"Would you care to see why Jasper was upset with your being here, Clint?"

"I'd care to see anything you'd care to show me, Miss Sultry."

She crossed the small room and opened the only other door in the room. It appeared to be a closet. She pushed the clothes aside, and Clint could see a door behind them. Sultry opened it, and Clint could make out a larger room beyond, and a canopied bed.

"My personal living quarters while I'm here at the El Dorado. We felt it too dangerous, even with Jasper as my bodyguard, to go back and forth to a hotel, since San Francisco is as it is. The two-way closet is a convenience."

"So I see."

"Would you care to take your coffee in there?"

Clint was amazed at how little he noticed his bumps and bruises as he crossed the room and followed Sultry into a satin, lace, and pillowed room that was about as pretty as anything Clint had ever seen — except for the woman who turned to face him, letting her wrap slide to the floor in a pile. Her black stockings and the corset with the red silk flower were barely visible in the dimly lit room.

Clint took a tentative step toward her, then stopped as she held out a hand.

"I want you to know that, though I have a number of men friends, Clint, none of them are allowed in here." She searched his eyes for understanding.

"I'm privileged," he managed.

Accepting that, she reclined across the soft down-filled counterpane, patting the place beside her.

"You are discreet? It's difficult enough for a woman who works in a man's world to keep her reputation. And I'd only allow a man here who would defend mine with his life."

"I won't say a word, even to my sainted mother."

Sultry smiled. "I should hope not." She reached to the bedside table and turned the lamp wick even lower.

She heard the thump of a boot hit the floor in the darkness.

"Tomorrow, when you have time to think on it, I'd like you to reconsider going to the gold country with me."

"That's for tomorrow," he said, and let the other boot fall to the floor.

CHAPTER SIXTEEN

Lucretia Banyon sat in her rocker, sewing up the rips in the girl's smock with practiced hands. Apolonia rested on the edge of the Banyons' bed, wrapped in a blanket. The door creaked open and Captain Isaac Banyon strode in.

"Are ye about finished with this foolishness, woman?"

"It is not foolishness for this girl to be properly clothed. If you will leave us, I'll be finished in short order."

Apolonia tucked even her bare feet up under the blanket and kept her eyes turned away from the captain. Grumbling, he closed the door, and she heard his footfalls moving away.

"Please, Señora Banyon, can you tell me why we are here?"

"Women are the evil business of this ship,"

Lucretia offered, not looking up from her sewing.

"I don't understand."

"This ship trades in women." Lucretia paused in her sewing, then stabbed fiercely into the ugly brown fabric. "Buys and sells them, like cattle or swine."

"And you . . . you condone this?"

Lucretia's voice softened. "I think it is the devil's work. It is an evil that begets evil." She bit off the remnants of a thread, then rose and crossed the room. "Here. I'm finished." Lucretia turned her back while Apolonia slipped the simple brown dress back over her head.

"Then will you help us escape?" Apolonia pleaded.

Lucretia looked away. "I would be going against my husband if I helped you."

Apolonia sank to her knees and took Lucretia's hand in hers, pulling it to her cheek. "If you are a Christian woman, you'll help us in the name of Christ. If you are not, you will help us because we are fellow women."

Lucretia jerked her hand away, but her voice caught in a sob. "I *am* a Christian woman. A woman who vowed to love, respect, and obey her husband. A holy vow in a Christian church, obeying God, not a papist edict from Rome."

Lucretia opened the door and shouted for her husband. Apolonia's hope waned as she heard his heavy footfalls in the passageway, then disappeared when the door opened and Banyon's frame filled the hatchway.

Captain Banyon clasped her wrist in an iron hand and began to lead her out. "We all worship the same God," she pleaded, her voice ringing down the hall. "All of us are made in His image. Help us, for the love of God."

Isaac Banyon worked the key in the padlock. "I should lash ye all for what ye've done," he said, and thought, *And I would, if it were not for my prying wife who awaits my return.*

Apolonia shivered, but said no more. The captain shoved the door open.

"Captain," she pressed, gaining enough courage to ask the question that had been burning in her. "You brought some men aboard? Men who were bound and gagged?"

"Not your business."

"But why are they here?"

Her voice sounded vulnerable and pleading, and so feminine. He thought of the girl's smooth bare breasts, and knew that he could never look at her again without remembering what he had seen. One answer would do no harm.

"They're conscripts. They've been brought aboard to fill out the crew." He shoved the door open and motioned her inside. "Now, ye best not cause any more trouble or ye'll taste the lash."

He slammed the door and moved back up to his cabin. Lucretia awaited him. She said nothing until he was seated and pulling off his boots.

"I will no longer be a part of this." She stood rigidly, her voice low, but her tone firm.

"I beg ye pardon, Madam?" Isaac paused, one boot in hand, one still on, and looked at her in astonishment.

"I have decided I will go ashore here in San Francisco and take a house. You will make this trip without me."

It was the answer to his prayers, but he knew better than to seem pleased. "Ye are sure this is what ye want?"

"Tomorrow we will go ashore and find a house."

"If it's what ye wish," he mumbled. "I may have to put my departure off a day to accommodate ye. But whatever makes ye happy, my dear." He did his best to sound as if she had just told him he was condemned to the gallows while fighting to hide the smile on his face. He removed the second boot and wanted to do a jig in his stockinged feet, but he restrained himself.

★ ★ ★

Gaspar Cota rested in the aft end of the ship, but his quarters were not as comfortable as even Apolonia's and the other women's. He and his three vaqueros lay chained in the stench of the dark bilge below Apolonia's room — a space tall enough only to crouch in. With the quiet roll of the ship, brackish bilge water, littered with the ship's refuse and an occasional floating dead rodent, lapped at their feet and legs.

They had not eaten in two days, not since they had been struck down and bound and gagged by the Sydney Ducks. Now, for the first time, they were ungagged and could at least talk among themselves.

"I know it was she," Gaspar lamented to Chato, his head vaquero and the *segundo* of the Cota rancho.

"But why would Apolonia Vega be on board a sailing ship?"

"Why was she abducted in the first place?" Gaspar snapped. "Tell me that, and I'll tell you why she's here."

Chato jerked on his chains for the hundredth time since they had been clasped on his wrists and ankles. "Well, *jefe*, now that we've come to her aid, maybe we can enlist hers."

"We will get off of this scum bucket," Gaspar said. "And we will take Apolonia with us."

★ ★ ★

By the time the sun warmed the streets, Gideon was already drinking his second cup of strong black coffee and awaiting his breakfast in the crowded Mariano's Cold Day Tavern. He squinted at the figure crossing the board-covered street outside, then chuckled as Clint came in. Leaning his Colt's rifle against the wall, he jauntily seated himself across the table.

"Top of the morning," Clint said.

"You're full of vim and vigor for a man who looks as if he was run over by a team of four and a beer wagon."

Clint self-consciously touched a bruise on his cheek, then smiled. "Nothing that a plate of Mariano's cackleberries won't cure."

"He's out of eggs again, but looks like he got a good do on the biscuits."

The fat Italian stuck his head out the door and looked questioningly at Clint.

"Ham, biscuits, gravy —" Clint said. "Hell, anything you got that won't bite back."

"Been bit enough, have you?" Gideon teased.

"Those boys weren't so tough."

"I wasn't talkin' about those boys." Gideon didn't smile, but his eyes took on a mischievous glint.

"How's a fella get a cup of coffee around

196

here?" Clint got up and fetched his own, ignoring Gideon's subtle inquiry, then returned to his seat. "Today's the big doin's at the Barracoon. You goin' over there with me to see the festivities?"

"I'm goin', but *festivities* isn't the word I'd choose." Gideon waited as Mariano set their plates in front of them and waddled back to the kitchen. "I know what it's like, being on the auction block. It's no fiesta."

"That girl, Su Chin, seemed eager to be sold."

"That girl has no idea what she's in for."

"After we've finished, let's go see for ourselves." Clint sopped at his gravy with a biscuit. "I've got all day to kill."

"Then what?"

"Then I'm paying a return visit to the crew of the *Amnity*."

"You're a glutton for punishment."

"Those boys took an unusual interest in me . . . and I think it's because I've been asking around about the missing Californio girls."

"That seems a long shot."

Clint took a draw on his coffee, draining it. "It would be, if the *Amnity* wasn't the ship that brought the China Marys here. A ship about to return to China, and I think her intent is to return with another load of women. Looks to me like Captain Isaac Banyon thinks he can conscript women with the same impunity he conscripts San Francisco drunks." Clint finished the last of his breakfast while Gideon mentally chewed on what he had been told. "I've got to take a look on board before she sails, and the dark of night would be the best time." Clint shoved back his chair. "You coming along to San Francisco's newest form of entertainment?"

Gideon pushed away his plate, leaving a good portion. "You couldn't keep me away with a team of draft horses."

Fifty China Marys stood on the raised platform in the center of the Barracoon. Though it was early morning and the auction didn't begin until nightfall, the place was already teeming with men eager to preview the goods.

For the first time, Su Chin began to feel like she had absolutely no control over her future. Her stomach seemed to house a thousand crawling scratchy-footed beetles and she trembled from her well-coiffed hair down to her silk-bound feet. Already she had been poked and prodded and commented about, as if she were not there, by dozens of leering, ugly, foul-smelling men.

Su Chin looked out over the crowd, her eyes searching for even one man she would consider a fit master. She had a mental picture of an eagerly bidding fine Chinese gentleman who needed someone to run his *gum san* household, or at worst, a wealthy white devil who would cherish an almond-eyed beauty and take her into his home and show her off like the treasure she was. Instead she looked out over a crowd of rowdy miners in calf-high boots, stained canvas pants, and rough shirts of jersey or homespun.

They milled around, made lewd remarks, spat vile gobs of tobacco juice on the floor, and eyed the women with hungry looks that would chill the stoutest heart. The Chinese who moved among them appeared no better. Fat, grasping, greedy-eyed men she feared would use the girls for far less noble means than running a household, or even serving as an honored concubine.

The men laughed, drank from one of the four bars centered on each wall of the big room, and commented on the cluster of women who stood on the platform, appraising them like sides of beef.

Scattered throughout the crowd was a select group of a dozen of General Zhang Ho's finest, largest, and best-trained Fu Sang Tong members. Big barrel-chested men dressed in black robes. All but one huge guard displaying no weapons other than ham-sized hands, they moved quietly through the growing crowd.

A wide thick-bladed sword with a two-handed hilt was carried casually by the huge guard. Its hilt was wrapped in red silk, and Su Chin knew, and feared its significance — the executioner's sword. She had seen, in China, many heads lopped off with a single swing of the heavy blades.

The last thing the general wanted was for his guards to be forced into using the tong hatchets or thin daggers each carried concealed under his robe.

Ho expected the preview and the auction to be carried out without any problem, and he'd instructed his guards to use the greatest discretion, especially with the white devils. He wanted no trouble with them; he wanted their gold.

As added insurance, he had hired ten white devils to also act as guards. Men specifically recommended to him by the city marshal's office, in addition to four deputy marshals the Fu Sang Tong had paid Marshal Larson to provide. The white devil guards were prominently displayed at each doorway and flanking the bars — and each carried a shotgun and wore a sidearm. They were identified with wide arm bands of white silk with an intricate *B* for *Barracoon* embroidered in bright Chinese red.

By the time Clint and Gideon had walked

the several blocks to the Barracoon, the long alley that ended at the front door of the big clapboard building was filled with men, and the street outside was crowded four deep with men watching a fistfight between two burly teamsters who bludgeoned each other over a place in line.

Clint and Gideon glanced at each other. Gideon shook his head. "What do you think Miss Su Chin thinks of being sold now?"

"Come on." Clint motioned him to the side street. "The hell with this line. We know a better way inside."

They circled the block, mounted the roof of the shop that backed up to the Barracoon, and pried the second-story shutter away. The building was so crowded that no one noticed when two men appeared out of the storeroom on the walkway above. All eyes were on the women.

As Clint and Gideon reached the bottom of the stairs, a lantern-jawed cigar-chewing guard at the end of the bar noticed them and walked over, his shotgun cradled comfortably in one arm. "No one is allowed upstairs."

"Suits me," Clint said, nodding politely to the man.

"What a bunch of vultures," Gideon said, looking out over the milling, leering crowd.

"Let's get a little closer." Clint began elbowing his way through the men, and Gideon stayed close behind. A rope had been strung between four-foot pedestals to keep the crowd out of grasping range of the women — though the men continued to broach it. It took several minutes, but finally Clint and Gideon reached the taut rope.

Su Chin saw them almost immediately. "You buy Su Chin . . . please?"

Before Clint could speak, a miner ducked under the rope and mounted the platform. With burly arms, he circled the shoulders of two of the girls. Standing between them, he smiled at his friends in the crowd, but two guards reached him and pulled him away from the women. They shoved through the crowd, pushing him toward the door. "I got money," he complained drunkenly, shaking his poke at them. "I got plenty of money and I aim to buy me a China girl."

The guards moved him to the door and outside.

"This could become a Donnybrook Fair," Clint cautioned while the crowd hooted and hollered after the man.

"Or worse," Gideon said quietly. "Much worse."

CHAPTER
SEVENTEEN

The crowd settled, Clint turned his attention back to Su Chin, who still watched them carefully.

Gideon shook his head slowly. "As beautiful as she is, that girl and this circus are the most pitiful things I've seen since I left Louisiana."

A group of men on Clint's right got into a shoving match over a table and chairs, and the guards yelled at them, pushing their way through the crowd. Clint moved away toward the wall. "Let's get off to the side and out of this gaggle."

As they passed the bar, Clint paused and ordered himself a beer and Gideon a soda water.

"I got no soda water," the bartender snapped. "I got some of this newfangled ginger ale . . . but it'll cost you same as if it had whiskey in it."

"Gimme the whiskey on the side," Clint said.

Clint turned to a miner leaning on the bar, passed him the whiskey, and received a tip of the hat in thanks. They moved on.

"You two are in the wrong part of town." The gruff voice stopped Clint short. "You remember me. I'm Vester Grumbles." The solidly built man sneered at them.

It was the man who had shot Henri LaMont. He held a shotgun in both hands, its barrels close to being leveled on Gideon. The muscles in Clint's shoulders bunched. Beside him he sensed Gideon about to move on Grumbles. Clint rested a hand on Gideon's forearm. The business end of a scattergun was nothing to trifle with.

"I didn't see a sign outside that said 'the wrong part of town,' " Clint said. "You saying we're not welcome here?"

Before Grumbles could answer, another man, dressed in a black robe and flanked by two thickset bodyguards, stepped in front of him.

"If you have gold in your pocket, Mr. Ryan, you're more than welcome here." Zhang Ho turned and said something under his breath to Vester Grumbles, who curled his lip at Gideon but turned and melded with the crowd.

The general returned his attention to Clint.

"I'm glad you have come, Mr. Ryan. I wish to talk with you in private, if you have time."

"I've got time," Clint said, glancing from Ho to his guards and wondering just what it was Ho wanted. He had thought about just what Ho's reaction would be to his showing up at the auction, after his uninvited visit.

Ho turned and headed for the stairway.

"You want me along?" Gideon asked.

"Damn right," Clint said without looking back.

Gideon followed Ho and the guards, who cut a wide path through the crowd.

Ho moved up the stairs and all the way down the walkway to the last door, where he motioned to his guards to wait outside. Clint followed Ho inside, but Gideon folded his arms and leaned against the rail. His brown eyes began a stare-down with the bodyguards.

Zhang Ho walked around to the back of a small oak desk centered in the barren corner office.

"You still seek the Californio women?" Ho asked.

"Yes. I have been employed to do so."

"By whom?"

Clint studied the man for a moment. He was the keeper of the Barracoon, and Captain Isaac Banyon's partner — but he was the only man who had ever mentioned the Californio girls without being prodded.

"I was hired by the family of one of the girls."

"I know where they are."

"On board the *Amnity*," Clint said quietly.

"You know?" Even Ho's inscrutable face registered some surprise.

"I guessed. I would have known soon."

"I will help you free them, Mr. Ryan. On two conditions."

"And those are?"

"It is imperative that the Chinese be cleared of any suspicion in these abductions, and almost as important to the Fu Sang Tong, it is imperative that Captain Banyon know nothing of my helping you."

"You're walking a fine line."

"Yes, but it's a path I must walk. It is critical to the future of the Celestials in the *gum san* that no one believe they are involved in such a thing. And you must relate to the authorities, and to the newspapers, that we were not. It is also critical to the tong that we maintain our partnership with Captain Banyon."

"How can you help me, then?" Clint sat on the edge of the desk.

"We will talk again tonight, after the auction."

"Good enough," Clint said, extending his hand and shaking with Ho.

For the first time he had a real break. Elated, he followed Zhang out the door. Gideon unfolded his arms and moved from his position on the rail.

The post next to him exploded in a shower of splinters and the room below reverberated with staccato gunfire.

Gideon dove forward into the bodyguards, who shoved him away. All of them realized at the same moment that the gunfire was not directed at them, and looked over the rail to the crowd below as it erupted in a clamorous riot.

Chairs and tables flew, bottles crashed, men cursed, and *mui gai* shrieked in terror. Knives flashed and guns roared.

Clint and Gideon charged down the stairs behind the bodyguards, but Ho cautiously backed into the office doorway, where he could watch in relative safety. He wrung his hands, fearing his business and profits were flowing away with the beer and blood below.

Clint jumped the last four stairs to the floor, where a burly cigar-chewing miner locked gazes with him and clawed for the pistol in his belt. The barrel of the Colt's flashed and thumped into the side of the man's head, the cigar flew, and he hit the floor.

Gideon spotted Su Chin on the platform among a group of grasping miners and screaming girls, her eyes wide with fear as a bearded miner reached for her. Gideon crossed the distance in three bounds. He poleaxed the man with a smashing right that knocked him out from under his slouch hat and sent him sprawling across the platform.

Gideon reached for Su Chin just as both barrels of a shotgun went off next to him. Stunned by the blast, he reeled, but the shot wasn't meant for him. A miner staggered on his heels, then fell like a timber near Su Chin's silk-bound feet, a knife still in his hand, but most of his chest blown away. Blood splattered across Su Chin's breast and she wiped madly at splotches on her cheek. Staring in revulsion at her bloodied hands, she wondered if it portended her future.

Gideon grasped her wrist and pulled her across his shoulder, then charged for the stairway, battering his way through the fighting men. His hat flew off and rolled away.

Clint and a teamster who held the jagged remains of a mug in his hand circled each other until Clint switched ends of the Colt's and used the butt on the side of the man's head. With a resounding thump, the teamster's eyes rolled back and he crashed unmoving to the floor.

Clint cut a path through the crowd toward Gideon. Using the barrel of the Colt's as a scythe, he led Gideon and his wide-eyed load to the stairs. They ascended halfway and Gideon set Su Chin down. He and Clint turned and started back into the melee.

They had moved only a few steps when the crowd quieted.

The huge Chinese guard had caught the attention of all by swinging the executioner's sword. It whistled through the air. When all turned to watch its fearful arcs, he brought it across a thick table, severing it like butter. It sobered every man in the crowd.

The guards had formed a line and moved into the crowd with shotguns leveled.

"Enough!" Zhang Ho shouted from the railing above. "You have seen enough of the girls. The auction will begin at sundown. Come back. Bring gold."

Grumbling, the men began to filter out. Deputy Thad McPherson and two other deputies, stars gleaming on their chests, burst in. Men holding bloody noses and knotted heads, carrying or allowing friends to lean on them, moved out into the alley.

Five men lay sprawled on the floor of the big room. One, whose chest was blown away, exposing his vitals, was obviously fodder for the undertaker. Another sat on the floor, leaning on one arm while his other hand grasped at his chest, where pink frothy blood bubbled from a knife wound. He moaned quietly, calling the name of some faraway loved one, though his throat gurgled blood. He would not live to see the auction.

Clint glanced upward to make sure that Su Chin was all right. Then he and Gideon began to move toward the door.

"You buy Su Chin, please, Javanese man?" she called down from the stairs.

Clint caught the look on Gideon's face — a grab bag of mixed emotions. He pulled his friend to the door.

Vester Grumbles stood close by, using the scattergun to prod the men along. "This yours?" he asked, and extended Gideon's high hat, smashed flat and covered with beer and mud. Grumbles snickered, but Gideon accepted it, popped it back into its proper shape, and fitted it in place on his head.

"Boss said to put the garbage out." Vester curled a lip. Reaching out with the shotgun, he poked Gideon in the ribs. "Outside," he managed, before Gideon wrenched the double barrel out of his hands and slammed it across his throat, pinning him to the wall.

Another guard, blond-headed and blotchy-faced, leapt forward, only to find the cold barrel of the Colt's rifle shoved under his wispy whiskered chin.

"Stay out of this," Clint warned, his eyes as cold and blue as new pond ice.

"You've pointed a gun at a LaMont for the last time," Gideon growled, nose to nose with the red-faced Grumbles.

Grumbles clawed for his sidearm, but Gideon slung the scattergun away, dropping a hand and catching Grumbles's wrist in a vise grip. Gideon brought his knee up with a crunching blow.

Vester lurched six inches up the wall. His red face went green, and his sidearm clattered to the floor. Gideon released him, and he slid slowly down the wall, grasping his groin with both hands. Gideon kicked the pistol away and it spun into the crowd.

Gideon snatched up the scattergun and the crowd reeled back as he swung it like a bat, bending the barrels across a post. He dropped it nonchalantly beside a retching Vester Grumbles, who had managed to get to his knees but was bent over, puddling the floor between his hands.

Gideon ambled past Clint and made for the door.

"We're going on outside now," Clint cautioned the blond-headed guard.

"Fine with me, friend," the guard replied, but his eyes were fixed on his fallen friend.

Clint caught up with Gideon, who took a deep cleansing breath as he stepped out into the crowded alley.

"I hate that place," Gideon said.

"And I get the impression you don't much like ol' Vester Grumbles," Clint said, a slight smile crossing his face.

"In a way that man did me a favor, shootin' Henri LaMont and setting me free, and he talks right about slavery." Gideon's look hardened. "But I can't abide a coward, and a backshooter is the worst kind. And that man even looks stupid."

For the first time since they had arrived at the Barracoon, Clint laughed out loud.

"I can't come back here, Clint," Gideon said, his eyes distant.

"Why not? So far you've cut a wide swath."

Gideon turned to him. "If I'm here, I'll spend every dime I've got to buy that girl."

"A fella could blow his money in worse ways."

"Maybe, but can you imagine me owning someone?"

Clint wanted to smile, but the anguished look on Gideon's face wouldn't allow it.

Instead he told him of his meeting. "Well, I've got to come back. Zhang Ho says the Californio women are aboard the *Amnity* and he'll help me get them off. On the condition that no one knows. I've got to meet with him again."

"Then I'm coming back with you. I'll just

212

ignore the auction."

"I'm sure you won't have to worry about it. Those women are going to go for big money."

Gideon didn't respond. He just kept walking.

CHAPTER EIGHTEEN

"I think it's beginning to widen," Chato whispered to Gaspar through gritted teeth.

He'd been jerking on the chain binding his right arm since the deck hatch to the bilge had been closed the night before. His wrist was gouged and bleeding. Still he jerked. The last length in the chain was slowly widening, an infinitesimal amount with each pull.

Suddenly he stopped. A shaft of light split the dank space and a voice echoed. "The captain said to bring you some gruel." Legs appeared at a deck hatch, and an old man dropped into the bilge, followed by another, younger form carrying a lantern in one hand and a bludgeon in the other.

The older man reached up through the opening and someone handed him a pot, some bowls and spoons, and a bucket. Then, awkwardly, he made his way across the ship's wooden ribs to the prisoners. The other man, a young Chinese, stayed well out of reach of the vaqueros, holding the lantern so the old man could work and a heavy belaying pin so he would be unmolested.

"I'm Abner Baggs, the supercargo of this fine ship and your jailer . . . until you take up your duties."

"How long are we to be kept in chains?" Gaspar asked.

"One of your hands will be released so you can relieve yourself and eat. Then you'll be chained again. You'll be set free after we're well out to sea. Then you'll take up the duties of a common sailor."

"When do we get out of this stinkin' bilge? Forcing a man to wallow in his own filth like a pig is inhuman."

"The bilge gets worse than yer paltry leavin's." Abner laughed. "We pump her clean every fortnight, less'n there be a storm at sea — then the pumps run day and night. But you'll soon enough have your turn at the pump handle."

Abner bent over Gaspar. "I'll be removin' the bolt from your right hand manacle. A slap at me'll cost you your grub and a kick — an' ol' Abner kicks like an Erie Canal mule. Any other tricks will cost you a knot on the head from Willie's belayin' pin." Abner began working at the bolt with a wide-mouthed wrench. "As you can see, these bolts is mighty tight and you'll never loosen one with yer hand. With Willie near, you'd have a head knotted like you stuck it in a hornet's nest long afore you ever got loose."

Gaspar merely grunted. He sighed in relief as the clasp clanked open, and he rubbed his wrist on his pants — but didn't get it near the other restraint. Abner began to work on Chato's clasp. Gaspar got to his knees, fumbled with his pants one-handed, and relieved himself into the bilge water.

"Look at that wrist, you fool." Abner chastised Chato as he worked on his bolt. "You can jerk against this chain like a coon in a trap until you tear that hand off, then Captain Banyon will feed it to the sharks and work you like you had two."

It was all Chato could do not to grab the old man by the throat and jerk his Adam's apple out. The old man hadn't noticed the link beginning to part.

Baggs released the other vaqueros, dipped up the gruel, and added a piece of salt pork to each bowl. The men ate in greedy silence. After drinking their fill from a bucket of water passed from man to man, they extended their wrists and the old man replaced the clasp bolts.

Isaac Banyon had risen with the sun as usual.

216

His night's rest had not been good and, even though elated with his wife's decision to remain in San Francisco, he was troubled. He would have to spend the afternoon and the evening at the Barracoon, protecting his interest and making sure he received his fair share of the profits. Consequently, he could not personally supervise the course of action he had decided upon during his night's tossing and turning.

Even though his first mate, Stoddard, had failed miserably in abducting Ryan, he was more than capable of the chore Banyon had in mind. A sea chore. Banyon spent the early morning hours carefully going over his instructions with Stoddard.

Lucretia also rose early. She had attended to her toilet and was dressed by the time Isaac left the room.

"I'll get my things together. When will we go ashore?" she asked calmly.

"Midmorning, if ye can be ready by then, dear."

"I'll be ready. I want to say good-bye to Mr. Stoddard and to Mr. Baggs and Mr. Docker."

"Mr. Baggs is going to accompany us into town. He has a few more supplies to gather. When ye are ready, come topside and ye can say your farewells while we load ye things."

She smiled tightly and nodded, and Isaac left. Immediately she went to Isaac's small rolltop desk, opened one of the tiny compartment doors, and removed a key. She didn't bother to put on her cloak. She hurried out, pausing to listen at the half ladder that led to the deck. Hearing nothing, she descended to the deck below and went straight to the women's door.

She knocked and heard the footfalls of someone hurrying to answer. "Yes."

"I want to talk to the young girl whose smock I sewed."

In a moment she heard Apolonia's voice. "Yes, Mrs. Banyon?"

"I'm going to open the door and I want you to step outside. Tell the other ladies to step back and give me no misery."

"They're back," Apolonia said anxiously.

The tumblers fell and the door creaked open. Cautiously, Apolonia stepped out.

Lucretia held the key between two fingers. "I want ye sworn promise that ye'll tell no one how ye got this."

"I swear."

"Ye must leave tonight. The *Amnity* will be at sea tomorrow or, at the latest, the next day. Then it will be too late for ye."

"Thank you." Apolonia hugged the key to her breast with both hands. Lucretia spun on her heel and made her way to the ladder. "God bless you," Apolonia called after her, staring at the small brass symbol of freedom as Lucretia's skirts disappeared up the ladder. She stepped inside the room and relocked the door.

By the time Isaac had returned from his meeting with Stoddard and his morning ship's rounds, Lucretia was packed. Two huge trunks and the rocker were tightly grouped in the center of the captain's cabin.

"Are ye ready, woman?"

"I'm ready, Isaac. I've made my peace." Isaac eyed her strangely, not sure what she meant.

But lately he was used to that.

Clint and Gideon stopped at Hardy's Livery on their way back to the El Dorado, where they had decided to wait until the Barracoon reopened. Clint looked Diablo over. The big horse reared and stomped and spun in the tight confines of the stall. He was either getting barn sour and didn't want to leave his stall, or there was a mare on the wind.

To make sure he would be well cared for, Clint tipped the stable hand, then spoke to the hostler, Hardy, about an extra ration of grain. Clint instructed him to have the stable boy exercise the big horse, agreed to an extra dime a day, then he and Gideon walked the next two blocks to the saloon.

The saloon, as usual, was packed. Clint strode to the bar, purposefully selecting the section where Luther Baggs worked.

"Mr. Baggs," Clint said, the sarcasm clear in his tone, "you need to treat your customers with a little more care."

"What's that supposed to mean?"

"That's supposed to mean . . ." Clint almost lost his temper, but didn't want to start trouble in the El Dorado. "That means you owe Gideon and me a drink."

"What the hell are you talking about?" Luther's bulldog brow crinkled as if he didn't understand.

Clint cut his wolf loose. He leaned forward, snatched Luther by the collar, and dragged him halfway across the bar. When he was nose to nose with the bartender, Clint's voice rang low and slow. "I got a passel of knots on my head on account of you lying about my friend here being drunk in the alley. Now, you can buy us that drink, or you can step out in the alley with us and we'll take turns teachin' you how to speak truthful."

Baggs grabbed Clint's wrist with one hand. His droopy eyes wide with fear, he cut them to Gideon, then back to Clint's steely gaze.

"I was only trying to help my pa," he mumbled.

Clint shoved him back across the bar. "While you're pourin' me three fingers of Noble's Finest whiskey, I'll tell you a story." Baggs hurried to get the backbar ladder so he could reach the highly placed bottle. Gideon and two strangers leaning on the bar listened with interest as Clint talked.

"An old farmer bought himself a mail-order bride. He took a mule-drawn buggy to pick her up, got hitched, and started back to his farm.

"That old mule acted up, and the farmer whipped him with a buggy whip, and said, 'That's one.' "

As Clint talked, Baggs poured him a generous glassful of the expensive whiskey and poured Gideon a soda water.

"Gideon will have a ginger ale," Clint instructed Baggs, then continued. "They went aways and the mule acted up again. The farmer climbed out of the buggy and hit that mule between the eyes with the butt of his rifle, and said, 'That's two.' His new bride looked at him with a jaundiced eye, but said nothing.

"The mule acted up one more time just as they turned into the farmer's gate. He jerked his rifle and shot the mule dead in his traces, and said, 'That's three.'

"The woman jumped up and said that was

the dumbest thing she ever saw a human do. The farmer stared at her a minute, then said, real quiet like, 'That's one.' "

Gideon and the two other fellows at the bar began to chuckle, but Luther looked puzzled. "What's that all supposed to mean?"

"Well, Luther, when you sent me out to the alley," Clint said, leaning across the bar, "that was one."

Luther blanched. Gideon picked up his ginger ale and toasted Clint. "Providential, Mr. Ryan." Then he turned to Baggs. "I hope you heard good."

"Good enough," Baggs managed sheepishly. He snatched up the bottle and topped Clint's whiskey off again. "On the house," he said.

The saloon quieted and Clint turned to the batwing doors. Sultry Mulvany, dressed in pink silk with a pink-feathered hat and matching Jenny Lind parasol, pushed through the doors. A few steps behind stalked Jasper Henry.

Sultry spotted Clint and the crowd parted as she walked to the bar. "Good afternoon, Mr. Ryan, Mr. LaMont."

"Ma'am." Clint took his hat off and smiled, feeling a warm pleasure at seeing her.

"I trust you two are having a pleasant morning?" As friendly as Sultry's smile was, Jasper Henry's frown more than offset it.

"We are now," Clint said, and the compliment caused Sultry's smile to widen even more.

"I'll see you later, Mr. Ryan." She spun her parasol over her head and moved away toward the stage. Jasper caught Clint's gaze and held it just a moment more than was polite.

"Good morning, Jasper," Clint said.

"Not to my way a thinkin'," Jasper said, his eyes searing into Clint. He spun on his heel and stomped after his employer.

After Jasper moved out of earshot, Gideon sidled up to Clint. "You've rubbed the salt in that ol' boy's scrapes about as deep as you should."

"I mean no insult to Jasper. In fact, I owe him a bottle of Noble's."

"Sometimes just being in the same state seems an insult to some men. Just watch out for him. He follows that woman like a dog, and there's nothing like a case of lace and lilac poisoning to make a dog go rabid."

"You fellas want another?" Luther interrupted.

"Yeah, a bottle," Clint said, and pointed at the Noble's. Luther produced it and Clint paid him. "Take it to Jasper. Tell him I appreciated the help. Can you handle that, Baggs?"

Luther nodded.

"Let's get something to eat," Gideon advised. "It may be a long night."

"Thank you, Mr. Baggs," Clint said politely, as if nothing had transpired between them.

They turned and left for Mariano's.

CHAPTER NINETEEN

Clint and Gideon stood in the long alley line to get into the Barracoon, for the word had been passed that no weapons were allowed inside; they would have to be checked with the guards at the door. The crowd, many of whom displayed the wounds of their earlier encounter, was subdued compared to the morning.

Clint handed over his Colt's rifle and pistol, a bit uncomfortable that the guards, including Vester Grumbles, still carried their scatterguns. Grumbles gave them a hard look but cut his eyes away when Gideon stared him down.

Four marshal's deputies, badges plainly displayed, were in attendance, including Thad McPherson, who caught Clint's eye and gave him a smile resembling one that a cat might give a cornered mouse. Clint tipped his hat.

The blood, beer and broken glasses,

smashed chairs, and tables, had been mopped up and removed. An auctioneer's podium rested on one end of the raised platform, and a roped-off walkway led to the stairs from there. A sign hanging near the entry door announcing CASH, GOLD, OR DRAFTS ON LOCAL BANKS ONLY was repeated in squiggly Chinese characters.

Clint spotted General Zhang Ho and approached him immediately. "Can we talk now?"

"After the auction, Mr. Ryan." Ho avoided meeting Clint's eyes. "We must not be seen talking. Meet me in the corner office after everything has quieted down."

Turning to go back to where Gideon had captured two chairs for them, Clint saw the reason for Ho's reluctance to talk. Captain Isaac Banyon stood against a wall, watching the growing crowd with interest.

Clint walked straight to him. "Captain Banyon, I believe."

"Mr. Ryan, isn't it?" Banyon's eyes narrowed, but he extended a sun-reddened hand that met Clint's.

"Are you bidding?" Clint asked, flashing a razor-thin smile.

"Hardly. I am owed a little money by the yellow devil who runs this affair. Are ye a buyer, Mr. Ryan?"

Clint ignored the question. "The rumor is that you're a partner in this meat market."

Banyon's jaw knotted. "That is a dirty lie. I'm an honest seafaring man."

Clint worried it like a cat with a near-dead mouse. "I may bid, but I prefer my women taller, and my Spanish is much better than my Chinese. You don't perhaps have any Californio girls coming under the gavel?"

Banyon's hands balled into fists, and his knuckles whitened. "Zhang Ho is the proprietor here. Ask him." Banyon spun on his heel, gave Clint his broad back, and shoved his way through the crowd.

Clint started back to his seat, but Thad McPherson stepped into his path, his gangly scarecrow body blocking the way. "Lazo, eh? I hear you go by Clint Ryan."

"I used to, before I came to California years ago. Now I use my Californio name, Lazo. Some still prefer Clint."

"You tried to cause trouble for a friend of mine "

"I don't call many backshooters friends," Clint snapped.

McPherson colored, his face almost the same red cast as his rumpled hair. He snarled, "You didn't come here on a brig called the *Savannah,* perchance?"

"I knew of her. Word was she went down

with all hands near Santa Barbara," Clint said, purposefully evading the question.

"Not all hands. Among other survivors, a fella name of Ryan, John Ryan, is still being sought in connection with the sinking. That fella wouldn't be you, now, would it?"

"My name is Lazo. It used to be Clint Ryan." Clint laughed and shrugged. "There must be ten thousand Ryans and Rileys and Kellys in the States from County Kilkenny alone."

"Well, Mr. Californio Lazo." McPherson's voice rang with sarcasm. "I haven't had a chance to sit down with Marshal Larson with this info yet, but I wouldn't be a damn bit surprised but what you'll have some real hard questions to answer, once I do."

"I'm not going anywhere," Clint said, "except over there to join my friend and watch these proceedings." Clint touched the brim of his hat and brushed past McPherson. As he crossed the room, he wondered how long it would take them to tie him together with John Ryan . . . John Clinton Ryan, his whole name. His time in San Francisco might be cut short. Wishing he had Apolonia Vega home and was on his way south to the shores of the Kaweah River, he found his seat.

"Well, look who's here," Gideon said, his eyes on the platform.

Clint glanced up to the podium, where Huly Up Hong stood next to the auctioneer. Dressed in black pants that matched the black collar and pocket trim on his bright red coat, the auctioneer rapped a highly polished cherry-wood gavel, quieting the crowd, then began to read out the rules of the auction. Hong translated into Chinese.

Not to be outdone, Hong wielded a gleaming black wooden striker and, leaning over a two-foot polished brass gong suspended from a mahogany frame in front of the podium, struck with abandon, gaining the total attention of the room. The second the room quieted, he began a slow repetitive beat and the first of the girls stepped out of a room above onto the walkway.

With the peculiar shuffling half walk, half trot of the Chinese, the girl descended the stairs and took the podium. Nervous, her eyes remained fixed on the floor. She was short, even for a Chinese, and her face shone almost white, with the help of zinc powder, and she was moon-faced — which was in proper proportion to her ample body. The auctioneer stepped toward her with a proud smile. Reaching out, he raised her chin like a father would show off a cherubic child.

"Pretty and chaste as the day she was born. And strong enough to launder and clean and"

— his eyes took on a lecherous gleam — "strong enough to satisfy all the other household needs . . . all night long, if necessary."

That drew an appreciative laugh from most of the men. Gideon fidgeted in his chair and looked at everything in the room but the now-quaking girl.

"Wish they would stop that damned dirge," he complained quietly to Clint, referring to the gong.

"Now, gentlemen, let the bidding begin." The auctioneer chattered and chided and worked the crowd, and to Clint's surprise, at the strike of the gavel, even this homely girl sold for a thousand dollars in gold. The slender hawk-faced man who purchased her had been pointed out to Clint before — he owned one of the worst pox-ridden brothels in town, and his face reflected the pocked memory of some dreaded disease. The girl would soon be ensconced alongside her Peruvian sisters.

The man paid in gold nuggets, and Zhang Ho carefully worked a fine set of glass-enclosed scales while Isaac Banyon stood a few feet away, pretending to watch the auction. Actually he was carefully noting each transaction on a piece of paper.

The bidding faltered for some of the girls who took the podium, going as little as four hundred for one who was butterball fat and sported a thumbnail-sized wart on her chin with inch-long black hairs dangling from it. But it mattered little to the fat Chinaman who bought her contract. He looked a little like a yellow warthog, shuffling and snorting as he excitedly paid for her with a melon-sized mound of silver Mexican pesos.

Gideon grew more taut as the bidding wore on, mopping his brow, grinding his jaw, shifting in his seat. Clint kept watch around the room. Thad McPherson leaned on a bar, his green eyes growing more the color of muddy pond water as he continued to knock down the free drinks the deputies had been allowed. Clint glanced to where Captain Banyon leaned against a wall, making copious notes. The wider Banyon's smile grew with the sales, the more furious Clint became, until a slow fire simmered in his gut. *The self-satisfied son of a bitch,* Clint thought to himself. Maybe he'd just scuttle the tub Banyon owned after he got the girls off.

Clint turned his attention back to the podium.

"Now we have the prize of the auction," the auctioneer began. "From the harem of a king." Hong did a roll on the gong that would be the envy of a fife and drum corp. All eyes turned to the smoke-hazed walkway, and whistles and cheers arose. Perched on a chair festooned with silk banners and affixed to two long poles, Su Chin was carried down the stairs by two of Ho's strongest guards, and the huge guard, displaying the executioner's sword, followed.

With regal aplomb, she was placed upon the platform and the red-coated auctioneer approached and gave her his hand. "An Oriental beauty of rare quality. A bird of paradise too beautiful to touch." He led her around the platform, demonstrating that she was mobile, even if only barely so on her bound feet. "The Chinese consider the binding of feet to be the ultimate in beautification.

"As you can plainly see, she can attend to all household duties." He cackled and the crowd came to life, whistling and shouting and stomping the floor until the dust rose.

He led her back to the chair, seated her, and stood in staged amazement at her beauty. Su Chin looked as if she were about to be cast into the lion's den.

He returned to his podium as Hong beat the gong. Su Chin kept her head lowered, her eyes searching the crowd with desperation.

"Now, gentlemen — and we would only allow this orchid to be sold to a gentleman." He paused. "But of course, the true measure of a gentleman is the size of his purse!" Clint scowled as this brought a laugh from every other man in the crowd, save Gideon, who mopped his brow and refused to catch the searching gaze of Su Chin.

"Now, who offers two thousand dollars to begin the competition?" The auctioneer waved his gavel around the room. He was asking for five hundred more than the top price of the day. For a moment Zhang Ho feared that all the high bidders had spent their gold and that he should have offered her early in the evening. Then the pock-faced Peruvian rose. "One thousand five hundred dollars."

The room buzzed. Then the noise increased as a tall, thin, graying Chinese, his silver queue extending from a high hat matching Gideon's, rose and spoke in singsong Chinese. Hong repeated. "One thousand six hundred."

"Another brothel owner?" Gideon asked with a low moan.

"I've never seen the man," Clint said. "But any man who put her in a brothel in San Francisco would have to buy a mule to carry his gold by the end of the first night."

Gideon looked ill.

"One thousand seven hundred fifty," the Peruvian shouted as soon as the room quieted enough so he could be heard.

Gideon stared across the room at the man, who looked like the grim reaper himself. "One thousand eight hundred dollars," Gideon called out, coming to his feet.

The room quieted. Then whispers blended and increased in volume like a beehive stirred with a stick, and quieted again. The auctioneer glared at Gideon. Finally he spoke. "You have the gold to meet such a bid?"

"I bid, didn't I?" Gideon's voice cut like sheet ice.

The bid by a black man seemed to encourage some and anger others. Within seconds the price rose to two thousand two hundred dollars. Then the bidding faltered.

The Peruvian stood and his eyes roamed the room. "Nothing but the best for my customers." He paused as dramatically as a Shakespearean actor. "Two thousand four hundred dollars." He sat back down casually, looking convinced that his jump would settle the matter.

Gideon rose again. "Two thousand five hundred dollars."

The Peruvian jumped to his feet, shouting over the clamor in the room. "I insist you make this man show you his gold."

The auctioneer looked at Gideon questioningly, but Gideon's eyes burned across the room to where the Peruvian stood.

"My mouth doesn't outweigh my purse, sir," Gideon stated flatly. "And any man who thinks it does better have fists like sledgehammers, or his blade sharp and his powder dry."

The Peruvian recanted his challenge by turning back to the podium. "Two thousand six hundred dollars." He grinned ghoulishly, as if the matter were finally settled, and took his seat. Noting the look on Gideon's face, the auctioneer seemed to agree.

"Going once." He raised his gavel.

With quiet desperation, Gideon whispered to Clint. "Do you have five hundred dollars?"

Clint still had not recovered from the fact that Gideon was bidding in the first place. "Five hundred dollars? You'll have me sleeping in the streets."

"Going twice," the auctioneer yelled over the din.

"Do you want to see Su Chin rot away with the lues?" Gideon asked, the question punctuated by the most agonized look Clint had ever seen.

"No, I don't, and yes, I got five hundred, but we'll both be out robbin' Chinese of their rice and fish heads tomorrow."

"Three thousand!" Gideon shouted triumphantly, and the room fell so deathly silent you could hear Zhang Ho rubbing his palms together.

"Damn," uttered the Peruvian.

Even the auctioneer gasped in shocked surprise.

"Three thousand?" the red-coated man repeated, recovering his composure. "Any other bidders?" With an anticlimactic plop of the gavel, he mumbled, "Sold. To the Ethiopian gentleman in the high hat and fancy suit."

Su Chin sagged in relief, closed her eyes, and sank into the festooned chair.

Gideon turned to Clint. "I hope you have that five hundred on you."

"I had five hundred," Clint corrected. "If my mathematics is correct, we paid about a month's wages per pound. I now own one sixth of a clubfooted China Mary. If I figure right, that entitles me to a leg and a rump."

For the first time since they had reentered the Barracoon, Gideon smiled.

"But not for long, my friend," Gideon said as he made his way past Clint and headed for Ho's scales. "Not for long."

Slightly confused by Gideon's statement, Clint followed along behind. Gideon's smile was only outshone by the normally inscrutable Ho's. Clint and Gideon untucked their shirts and removed money belts. Clint's Spanish reals joined Gideon's much larger pile of double eagles on the scale plate.

Clint wondered what Gideon had meant by "not for long," but now nothing Gideon would do could surprise him.

CHAPTER TWENTY

After Ho completed assigning Su Chin's indenture contract to Gideon and Clint, they headed for the platform, where Su Chin remained seated. Behind them the crowd of men filed out of the Barracoon — a few of them smiling, with *mui gai* in tow.

Clint and Gideon made their way under the rope and stood before her. She glanced up at Gideon, then bowed her head. "I your servant."

"Only until we can find a lawyer," he said gently. She looked up in surprise.

"What mean?"

"I will set you free of your contract. Maybe someday you'll be able to repay Mr. Ryan and myself the money we *loaned* you."

Clint was not surprised. He said nothing, just watched quietly.

"How Su Chin get along?" she asked, her

face a jumble of mixed emotions.

"Su Chin is a clever and beautiful girl," Gideon said softly. "I too was chattel, and I'm doing fine as a freedman. You will find a way. I have a few more dollars to advance you until you figure out how to get by."

"Hell, I've got fifty more," Clint said, seeing how frightened the girl was. "You can borrow half of it."

Gideon flashed him a grateful smile. "Then you'll have almost a hundred dollars. If you're careful, you can live for three months on a hundred dollars, even at San Francisco prices. That'll give you a good start."

"When must Su Chin repay? What interest?" she asked quickly.

"When you can. I want no interest," Gideon said, glancing at Clint for confirmation. Clint shrugged his shoulders.

"Not fair," she said. "Four percent per month?" Her face faded to the cunning blankness of a natural-born negotiator.

"It's not necessary," Gideon said.

"Four percent?" she repeated. That was less than half what the market would bear in San Francisco.

Gideon glanced at Clint and again received only a shrug of the shoulders. He turned back to her. "If you insist. I'll have the note drawn at four percent."

Clint watched the girl and suddenly felt at ease. He had already written the five hundred off as a cost of friendship, but now had no doubt that he would be repaid in full, with interest.

Su Chin extended her hand to seal the bargain. Gideon took the slender soft palm and smiled broadly. A tear glazed her cheek, leaving a track in the zinc powder she had used to whiten it. Knowing it was a tear of joy, Clint chuckled until Gideon turned to him.

"I don't know what the hell I'm laughing about," Clint growled. "We'll all be sleeping in the stall with Diablo tonight."

"You and I, maybe. She'll have a room and a bed and no by-God keepers chaining her to it while some pox-ridden sailor passes Satan's burden on to her."

"That sounds right to me," Clint said. He noticed Captain Isaac Banyon crossing the almost vacant Barracoon to where Zhang Ho and his Fu Sang guards were bagging the money in three heavy canvas sacks, each of which would have held twenty pounds of grain. Clint moved to where three miners stood finishing their drinks. Acting as if he were part of the miners' conversation, he listened to Ho and Banyon.

". . . and by the gods, that wasn't the bargain," Banyon was saying, his face slightly red.

"I will make the settlement in the morning, Captain," Ho said placatingly, backed up by several of his guards. "I must have time to account for all of the expenses. Then we will split the proceeds as agreed. You are welcome to remain here in the Barracoon with the money and my guards if you so desire."

"I will sail, with my share of the gold, on the afternoon tide tomorrow. Do ye understand?"

"I assure you, the accounts will be complete long before you raise anchor." Ho's tone left no doubt that he meant what he said. "And you will have your half as agreed."

"I'll be here at first light, and the money had best be here, too, or I'll track ye heathen hide to the ends of the earth. My crew will be usin' yellow skin to scour the decks." Banyon spun on his heel and stomped for the alley door.

Clint immediately went to the stairway and made his way up, catching Ho's eye as he did so. Ho nodded in acknowledgment. After giving the guards instructions, Ho ascended the stairs, with one of his burly guards close behind. The hired white guards and the two remaining marshal's deputies filtered back into the Barracoon from the alley.

Clint followed Ho into the office, while the guard waited outside.

On the platform below, Gideon glanced uneasily at the way the twelve white guards were dispersing themselves around the room.

Vester Grumbles stood beside Thad McPherson and another deputy, chatting and laughing. Still, the way two of the white guards approached the deputies from the rear made Gideon tense. Then the pieces fell in place. He jumped up and yelled, "Look out!"

But it was already too late. One of the white guards clubbed McPherson from behind with the butt of his shotgun. McPherson slammed to the floor. Grumbles shoved his shotgun into the belly of the second deputy. Another guard slammed a gun butt into the back of the deputy's head, and the deputy joined McPherson out cold on the floor.

The Chinese guards, at first confused, drew their hatchets from under their robes, and the huge guard with the executioner's sword stood in front of all of them, its arcs whistling a warning.

Grumbles glanced over at Gideon. "I'll get to you later." He laughed aloud and joined his shotgun-toting companions, who closed in on the Chinese. Like a stand of black oak tree trunks, the Chinese gathered around the sacks of gold in a semicircle. The white guards stopped a dozen steps from them.

"Now, what do you Chine'e boys think

you're gonna do with those little excuses for axes an' that meat cleaver?" Grumbles said with a sardonic laugh. "Let me show you what a real weapon will do." The shotgun bucked and spat flame, and the largest of the Fu Sang guards flew back against the wall, his arms and legs splayed out, his chest a pattern of bloody slug holes, and the executioner's sword spun away uselessly. He slowly slid down the wall, leaving a smear of blood.

Clint and Ho, deep in conversation behind the closed office door, hoped the shot they heard had come from outside. When they realized it hadn't, Clint scrambled for the door.

Gideon scooped up Su Chin and placed her behind the low platform, out of Grumbles's line of fire. "Don't move," he cautioned her. His right hand snaked behind his back, under his coat, and reappeared with Grumbles's own Root's Patent Model. Shoving both hands in his coat pockets, the Root out of sight, he climbed back up on the platform, an interested nonparticipating observer.

Clint flung the door open and took in the scene at a glance. His jaw clamped — his Colt's rifle and pistol were checked at the door below.

He glanced around the office for a weapon, any kind of a weapon. From the desk drawer, Ho drew two of the prettiest nickel-plated

Patterson Colt's Clint had ever seen. Ho tossed them both to him. "They are loaded, but I have never fired them," he said.

Clint stepped out of the door and caught the glint of the hatchet held by the guard who had followed Ho upstairs. The white guards below moved forward, gesturing with the scatterguns, and the Fu Sang retreated from the money bags. The guard on the walkway swung his hatchet in a full arc and flung it. Clint stood hypnotized by its keening whistle, watching the blade spiral end over end, then slam into the back of one of the white guards below.

The response was instantaneous. Half a dozen shotguns cut loose at the walkway above. The big Chinese slammed against the wall with half a hundred pellets in his chest, with such force that he bounced back over the railing and spun head over heels to the floor below.

Clint dove back in the office. The white guards fired at him and splinters from the doorjambs splattered through the room.

"Jesus," Clint swore.

He cocked both Colt's and leaned through the doorway, snapping off two shots before the wall exploded with a burst of splinters again.

Three of the white guards hefted the money

243

bags, and Grumbles yelled to the others to keep Clint in the office. He followed the three carrying the money toward the door, then realized that Gideon stood on the platform, taking it all in as if watching a stage show.

Vester Grumbles paused at the edge of the platform, a sadistic smile curling the corners of his mouth. "I shouldn't waste one of these loads on your black ass, but then again, why not?" He raised the shotgun just as Gideon's coat pocket pointed at him and exploded. Grumbles's eyes stared vacantly when he hit the floor, a perfect round .31-caliber hole between them.

Gideon dove off the platform and covered Su Chin with his body, pressing her to the floor. The edge of the platform and the chairs behind where they hid were blown apart. The room roared with shotgun fire.

With the distraction, Clint dropped to the floor of the walkway and began firing both Colt's alternately. Four of the white guards sprawled on the floor, but the three with the money reached the doorway. One of them did a forward somersault and dropped his money bag, a .31-caliber hole in his spine. Five of the guards, empty-handed, reached the rear door of the Barracoon, but two of them fell to Fu Sang Tong hatchets before they made it out.

The last of the guards, only one load in his shotgun, ran past Thad McPherson, who, groggy from the blows, struggled for his revolver. The guard gave him the remaining load, blowing away McPherson's face as he passed.

Clint tracked the guard with the Colt's in his right hand. The gun bucked, and the man spun. Another shot from Gideon's .31 took him in the throat.

But two bags of money were gone.

The room hung heavy with the smell of gunpowder. Clint panned the Colt's, seeking another target. Moving down the walkway, he descended the stairs to where Gideon was rising from behind the shelter of the platform. Su Chin wisely made no move to get up.

Ho reached the bottom of the stairway just behind Clint and looked around at the carnage. Four of his guards lay on the floor holding ugly gaping shotgun wounds. One lay dead, his chest raw meat and shattered bone. Eight white devil guards sprawled around the room, along with two marshal's deputies. Clint and Gideon moved from guard to guard, making sure that those who were only wounded had no weapons. Low moans filled the room.

Su Chin looked up at Gideon as he reached down for her. He had decided to get her out of the blood-splattered room — at least as far as the alleyway. "Can go now?" she asked, her eyes wide.

"We can go outside, Su Chin, but we can't leave quite yet," Gideon said, a gentle smile on his face. "We'd better wait there for the marshal. He'll want some answers. Then we'll get you to a hotel."

"As wish," she said, and managed to pick herself up off the floor onto the edge of the platform.

Clint walked over to where Ho stood, wringing his hands. "They got away with two bags of money."

"This is terrible," Ho said. "As part of our bargain, I was responsible for the girls after they arrived — for their safety, and for the money's. There will be enough to pay Captain Banyon for his share of the profit. The loss will be ours. We must get our money back."

He waved what was left of the Fu Sang guards over and gave them quick instructions in Chinese. They disappeared out the door, one remaining behind and taking up a watchful position near Ho.

"Can you help us get the money back?" Ho asked. "I will pay handsomely."

"I've got a job to finish first. Then I can," Clint assured him. "I'll be back as soon as I finish with the *Amnity*."

"Of course. Do your job . . . but you could

be of service to the Fu Sang while you are at it. If Captain Banyon were to die, that, too, would be to the tong's benefit, under the present circumstances."

"Not my line of work," Clint snapped.

"Still, you will help recover the money?"

"I'll come back, and we'll talk about it."

"Don't you think we should wait for Marshal Larson?" Gideon asked.

"No time," Clint said. "You can, but I'm gonna make this thing with the Californio women end."

Gideon turned to Su Chin, loaned her an arm, and guided her to the door.

Clint recovered his own weapons from a closet used as a checkroom, and followed out the door into the darkness.

"You never mentioned that nasty little belt gun," Clint chided Gideon as they moved down the dark alley.

"Never felt the need to. Never thought I'd have to pull it. 'Sides" — Gideon smiled in the darkness — "I didn't have much time to practice and you shouldn't depend on a fella who's not much of a shot."

"Yeah, I noticed that," Clint said facetiously. "You blew a hole in a good suit."

After a few steps, Gideon realized they would be half the night walking at Su Chin's pace. With a broad smile, he swept her up into his arms and followed Clint's brisk stride.

Within the hour they had Su Chin situated in a room — Sultry Mulvany's. She agreed to let the girl stay until they could find a house for her the next day.

While they headed for the wharf and the *Amnity,* Clint explained to Gideon what information he had received from Ho during their short meeting before the shooting had started. Willie Boy Wong was to be their contact on board the ship. If they could find him before the other sailors discovered them, he would help them locate the women.

The two men made their way through the quieting late-night streets of the city. Around them, men without rooms camped in the streets, fires burning near their bedrolls, stock tethered nearby. They walked to Front Street, then to the end of Long Wharf, where the quiet was interrupted by a group of men enjoying a song played on pan pipes and a fiddle, and stared out into the bay.

At first Clint thought his eyes were deceiving him. Then he walked over to the group of sailors who warmed their hands at a small fire built in a whaling ship's try-pot, only one of the thousands of nautical items — coiled line, ricking, rigging, and sails — that cluttered the wharf.

"Where's the *Amnity?*" he asked. The players laid their instruments aside and one of the listeners glanced up. "The *Amnity?*" Clint repeated. "She was anchored out there." He pointed to the vacant spot among the many ships.

"She moved out on the afternoon tide," the sailor muttered, returning his attention to the fire.

Clint's mouth went dry. Beside him, the men took up a lively chanty.

CHAPTER
TWENTY-ONE

The afternoon tide, the man had said.

Clint stayed silent as he and Gideon made the dark climb through the quiet streets back up from the bay to the El Dorado. The *Amnity* sure as hell didn't leave without her captain. And Banyon had been at the Barracoon until well into the night. No, she was still in San Francisco Bay. But where? The bay, including its sister bay, San Pablo, lay over fifty miles long and ten miles wide in spots. There were over a hundred and fifty miles of shoreline, not to speak of the three major islands lying inside the Golden Gate. He cursed himself for not acting sooner. She could be anywhere.

The *Amnity* had to leave via the narrow Golden Gate, but standing on Telegraph Hill watching her leave would do him little good. All he could do was wave good-bye — good-bye to the Californio girls and any hope of returning Don Vega's daughter to him. Good-bye to the promised Andalusian brood stock. And probably good-bye to his hopes for a ranch.

Clint shoved open the batwing doors to the El Dorado, and he and Gideon shouldered their way through the crowd. Luther Baggs leaned against the bar, on the customer side, talking to his father, Abner Baggs — the su-percargo of the *Amnity.*

"The saints are smiling upon me," Clint said, half under his breath. He and Gideon bellied up to the bar beside the two men.

"Your night off, Luther?" Clint asked with a smile. "I owe you a drink."

Luther eyed him suspiciously when Clint waved the bartender over, ordered a Dog's Head ale and a ginger ale, and told him to bring Luther and Abner whatever they were drinking. He flinched as the man took the five-dollar gold piece he handed him and returned him only three dollars. The twenty-five dollars he had left after Gideon's experiment in eman-cipation was already down to twenty-three, and that would go fast at this rate.

"Luther tells me you're serving aboard the *Amnity?"*

"Aye, and a fine vessel she is."

"I noticed she's hauled anchor. I'm sur-prised to see you here."

"She's not far, friend. Thanks for the drink." Abner toasted Clint, then gave him his back and continued his conversation with his son.

"Why'd she move?" Clint pressed.

Abner glanced over his shoulder. " 'Cause Captain Banyon ordered it. Are you with the newfangled city harbor commission, lad?"

"Hardly," Clint said with a feigned laugh. "Just interested."

"Well, to tell the truth, I don't know where she lies at the moment. I'm waiting for her master. Then we'll be off to the *Amnity,* and off to the shores of the Orient."

"To a good voyage!" Clint raised his glass. When the old man resumed his conversation with Luther, Clint whispered to Gideon. "We'll find her soon enough, if we can stay close to this old salt."

"Best we not be afoot," Gideon advised. "I'll fetch your horse and rent myself one while you keep an eye out." He upended his drink and left the bar at a brisk stride.

Clint moved away from Luther and the old man and found a spot near Jasper's pianoforte where he could listen to the bald-headed man's rambunctious pounding, but still see his quarry.

Jasper didn't take time from his playing to thank Clint for the bottle of Noble's, but did manage to shoot him a baleful glance.

It was a good thing Gideon left in a hurry, for shortly after he had gone, Isaac Banyon's ample frame entered the saloon. Clint glanced away as Banyon surveyed the room. If Banyon noticed Clint across the smoky distance among the hundred or more customers, he gave no indication. Rather, he moved directly to the bar. Clint hoped he'd pause long enough for a last drink before he headed out to the ship, but he didn't. Instead he spoke sharply to Abner, who quickly shook hands with his son. Then the two sailors strode out the door.

Clint hustled to the batwings, ignoring the insults of the men he elbowed aside, in time to see the two climb into a poor copy of a hansom-style cab with a shimmering whale-oil cut-glass lamp on either sidewall, pulled by a big dappled gray horse. The driver sat at the rear and above the body of the cab, over-looking it and the animal. Behind and below his perch, demonstrating frontier practicality, hung a low leather boot for luggage.

Clint squinted into the darkness, hoping to see Gideon and the horses. Then the cabby cracked his whip over the gray and the carriage started away with Clint's hopes.

Clint ran for the cab, caught the leather straps of the boot with both hands, and managed to swing his feet under and rest them on the single axle. It was uncomfortable and straining, but as long as he wasn't seen by the driver, he could hold on for a short trip.

The handler whipped the gray into a trot. A group of boys in the light of a shop window pointed at Clint and laughed as the carriage clattered past on the board-covered street, but the driver paid them no mind. Clint wound his arms into the straps, giving himself a firmer grip. The cabby had to rein up to allow a dray through an intersection.

"Here, now!" a voice rang out from the boardwalk as the cab clattered by a whale-oil streetlamp. "Driver," the meddlesome voice shouted. "You've got a freeloader!"

Clint cringed when the cabby looked over his shoulder, but apparently seeing nothing awry, he went back to his job. Clint could see the back of the man's head and the tail of his whip on its backstroke.

The cabby must have had an afterthought. He leaned back and looked down. Before Clint could unwind his forearms and avoid the cabby's wrath, the whip lashed down and caught him across the face. He dropped away, skittered across the boards, and rolled into the gutter, hearing the curses of the cabby, who shook his fist and disappeared into the darkness. Clint's stomach churned. The cab and his hopes for Apolonia Vega and the ranch disappeared into the darkness.

Apolonia and the girls had been ecstatic when Lucretia Banyon had brought them the key. They planned carefully, assessed their mistakes from the earlier attempt, and decided upon the course of action that they would take just as soon as it was dark.

Then they had heard the capstan being manned by six able sailors, and the anchor chain clattering aboard. The women stared at each other in panic in the dimness of their little room and wondered if they had waited too long.

"Should we run on deck and jump into the water?" one of the girls asked.

"Don't be silly," Juanita Robles snapped. "None of us can swim and we would only drown or these brutes would hook us out of the water like fishes."

"Then what do we do?"

"You will wait here," Apolonia said. "I will sneak out and try to find our men."

"No," Juanita said sharply. "Not until it's dark. If they find you, they will want to know how you got out of the room, and that key and surprise are our only hopes."

"Then I will go when it is night."

After several hours, just about the time it was good and dark outside, they again heard the clattering of anchor chains and felt the ship come to a shuddering halt.

They looked at each other in relief.

"How far do you think we've gone?" Apolonia asked.

"A few hours only. I would guess we are still in the bay."

"Good. Then we still have a chance. If only I can find where they have kept Gaspar and the others, we will soon be free."

Harlan Stoddard liked the feel of being the master of the ship, at least as long as Banyon was gone. He was pleased with his relocation of the *Amnity* to Hunter's Point. No one could have done it better. In fact, he thought, as the anchor chains were secured and he released the men from duty, he was so pleased that he would treat Mr. Vandersteldt to a drink.

He headed for the officers' galley, aft on the same level as the captain's cabin, and yelled at the second mate, Vandersteldt, to join him.

Yes, it had been a fine sail, if a short one. And it would be a fine voyage, now that Lucretia Banyon was ashore. Stoddard had never approved of having a woman aboard a vessel. A hen ship, the *Amnity* was known as while she had a woman aboard. It was demeaning.

A drink would suit him fine, in celebration

256

of his flawless command of the ship and of Banyon's getting rid of the pious woman. Hell, Banyon might even be fit to live with now.

"Damn the flies," Clint grumbled, climbing to his feet and brushing himself off, wondering if he could possibly keep up on foot.

"Mount up!" Gideon shouted, galloping out of the darkness, leading Diablo. "I tried to stay far enough back so they wouldn't see."

A resurgence of hope rushed through Clint. He slapped Diablo on the rump and mounted, swinging into the saddle without the use of the stirrups. Within seconds they had the side lamps of the carriage in sight.

They crossed Market Street, passed through the residential area south of it, and were soon out of town on the wagon road south to San Jose.

"It was a damn good thing you caught up," Clint said to Gideon, who trotted his buckskin alongside on the wide rutted road. "They're turning."

He could see the flickering lights of the carriage leave the road. They slowed, giving the cab time to get well into the grove of sandpaper oaks, then followed a narrow wagon path east. The night was starlit, with the hint of a fingernail moon just appearing across the bay. They cleared the oaks and crested a sand dune. A village of a few Chinese huts lay near the water. They reined up and watched as the cabby drew rein near one of the hovels.

Beyond the village, a quarter mile out into the bay, the *Amnity*, only one anchor lantern glowing, lay dead still in the quiet water.

Clint exhaled a sigh of relief, then realized his problems were just beginning.

CHAPTER TWENTY-TWO

Apolonia eased the cabin door open and stood listening to the silence in the lower passageway. She stepped out, closed the door, and locked it behind her. She knelt and searched her garment until she found a loose stitch, then hid the key in the hem of her smock. Making her way carefully along the passageway, she felt her way along, arms spread from wall to wall. Pausing, she listened at two other doors, tried the locked handles, and whispered, "Gaspar!"

Nothing.

She saw no light from the rooms, nor heard any sounds.

Starlight filtered from the deck hatchway on the level above and offered some light, but little comfort. She looked upward, her palms cold and wet, her mouth dry.

Taking a deep breath, she calmed herself

and mounted the ladder. She climbed until she could peek into the level above. Lantern light filtered out of a louvered door into the passageway. She topped the ladder, then tiptoed forward.

Gruff laughter hit her and she reeled back, almost stumbling, but she made little noise and the laughter continued. Trying to be silent, she took several deep breaths until her heart stopped pounding so hard. She moved deeper into the passageway and paused at a second door, across and farther aft. No light came through its louvers, but someone might be sleeping inside.

Her hand found the cold brass handle. It opened. The door behind her creaked and light flooded the hallway. With a leap she darted inside the dark room and shoved the door shut. More noises outside, then quiet. When she peeked out the door, the flood of light was gone. Her chest beat like a kettle drum, and her ears rang with the pounding.

She surveyed the room. Two large portholes graced the large cabin. *This must be the captain's,* she thought. She made a mental note of its contents — a four-poster bed, a desk with brass lamp and chair. She moved to the desk and, unable to make out the items on the top, rifled her hands over it. She tried the drawers and felt around for a weapon.

Nothing. Then something sharp pricked her finger and she pulled a foot-long wooden instrument out and examined it while she sucked at the tiny wound. The wooden arms of the device were connected by a wing nut at one end and needle-sharp two-inch metal points at the other. Points sharp and long enough to serve as a weapon.

She hurried back to the door, found the cold brass again, and eased out. Stepping onto the ladder to move up to the deck, she caught a glimmer out of the corner of her eye. The laughter from the lighted room had become an argument. She was afraid they would leave the room again.

She ascended the half ladder to the deck on cat's paws, clasping the weapon tightly, then stepped out into the night. A gentle breeze caressed her cheek and she realized how much she hated being locked up below. Light threw flickering shadows from a lantern on the quarterdeck over the aft end of the ship. She could hear singing and instruments being played somewhere forward, where she guessed the crew must sleep. A lively sea chanty rang from their quarters.

At another time and place, she might have enjoyed it.

Where would Gaspar and the others be? She heard a man cough, near where the light came from, and she ducked back out of sight. She moved quickly down the ladders to the lower level and stood in the dark passageway, searching her mind.

The men had come aboard bound. They were prisoners. Male prisoners would not be treated nearly as well as the women. They would most likely be locked up somewhere. The hold? But how to get into the hold? She knew it must be the greatest portion of the ship. The massive center area between the captain's and officers' cabins aft and the fo'c'sle forward. She also knew that the deck of a ship she had visited long ago had huge hatchways located in the main deck itself that opened into the hold.

But she could never manage to move one of those big, heavy hatches.

There must be another way.

As her eyes adjusted to the almost total darkness of the passageway, she caught a faint glint from the wall forward of the ladder. Since the hallway stopped there, the hold must be beyond. She ran her hand up and down the bulkhead and felt the coldness of brass in two spots. Hinges? She moved her hand away from them an adequate distance and felt a rush of hope. A let-in metal latch! Fumbling with it, she moved it, and the cover swung in.

She ducked inside. Though it was totally

dark in the space she entered, she pushed the cover closed behind her. Dropping to her hands and knees, she felt along the rough unfinished deck to determine the size of the space. The area was cold and dank, and a shiver racked her. She crawled faster, the space being larger than she had imagined. Then her hand shot into an opening where the deck should have been and she fell heavily to her chest.

"Who's there?" a voice called out in Spanish.

She collected herself and listened but heard no more. Finally she gathered her courage and ventured a reply.

"Apolonia Vega."

"Thank God. You are all right?"

"Gaspar . . . Gaspar Cota?"

"Yes. We are chained in the bottom of the hold. You are above, on a sort of balcony overlooking the main hold. Do not try to come down. It is too dangerous in the darkness. We need a tool, a wrench, in order to loosen our manacles."

"I have a tool . . . a sort of spreading tool with sharp points. I found it on the captain's desk."

"They are dividers, used for measuring distance on charts. Useless. We need a wrench for loosening bolts."

263

"Where would I find such a tool?"

"I don't know. Chato has freed one hand. He can work the wrench and we can all be free, if only you can find one."

"I will try," Apolonia said, her voice wavering. Somehow the sound of a familiar voice made her feel suddenly vulnerable and helpless and very, very frightened.

"I will try," she repeated. *I must try,* she convinced herself, bolstering her courage. She turned to crawl back to the cover. In a few seconds she found it, and her strength and bravado returned with the dim light of the passageway.

Now to find a tool.

Clint and Gideon sat astride their horses, watching the carriage deposit the captain and his supercargo. Banyon paid the driver and the cab wheeled around. Clint reined away from the road and led Gideon over a sand dune. They waited until the cab passed, then reined nearer to the Chinese hovels.

The moonlight glimmered across half a dozen mud and pole shacks, which squatted just above the bay's high tide line. Nets and cork floats hung drying, draped across the rounded huts. An interwoven willow-pole rack, eight feet square and high, arched over a two-foot-deep pit smoldering with glowing ash. The rack was shingled with hundreds of flat round petrale sole absorbing the rising smoke and emanating an oily haze that permeated the night air.

Clint could see Banyon near the open door of one of the shacks, backlit by a lantern, negotiating with a Chinese fisherman. Soon the man led him and Baggs to a small fishing boat among several that had been dragged high up on the mud flat. All three of them fought to get the boat into the water.

"If we got rid of those two now, we wouldn't have to deal with them later," Gideon advised.

"True enough, but the shooting would alert those on board. I think it's better we wait and catch them all unawares."

"We might not have to shoot."

"But then again, we might, or they might. Not worth the risk."

They waited patiently while the Chinese sculled the little boat out to the *Amnity,* then sculled back. The night was clear, but mist was beginning to rise from the mud flats and soon, Clint hoped, it would be foggy. Clint approached the Chinese fisherman at the beach while Gideon hid the horses among the sandpaper oaks. Clint stopped the fisherman before he could drag the boat out onto the mud. Another quick negotiation, aided by Clint's ability to speak some Chinese, and Clint and

Gideon were aboard the tiny catboat.

Harlan Stoddard, in the officers' mess, sat back in his ladder-back chair and glared at Vandersteldt, who with a pained look on his face rubbed his right bicep, then the burned back of his hand.

"You'll never beat Stoddard of the steel arm," Stoddard chided the Dutchman he had just mercilessly bested at arm wrestling. To make things interesting, he had placed candles where the loser would snuff the flame with the back of his hand. Stoddard had sadistically held Vandersteldt's hand over the candle when he could have easily driven it down and ended the contest.

The door to the officers' mess burst open. Captain Isaac Banyon filled it, eyes wide, nostrils flaring. Behind him Abner Baggs stood on tiptoe to look over his shoulder. Harlan Stoddard, a half-empty mug in his hands, faced Marvin Vandersteldt across the table. Both men were obviously in their cups.

"Damn ye, Harlan Stoddard," Isaac spat. "I cannot leave ye for a day without ye gettin' into the grog."

"You weren't due back until dawn," Stoddard growled back, his words slurred.

"Aye, but that damnable woman of mine wanted to spend the nighttime hours reading

266

me the Scriptures, rather than the way a woman should treat a man about to set sail on a long voyage."

"But we've seen the last of her," Stoddard said with a tone that irritated Banyon. Even more irritating was his question. "Did it go well at the Barracoon?"

"We're heading back in the morning. You and half the crew to accompany me — well armed and ready to burn the damnable place if I'm not satisfied with the divvy."

"That crafty Chinaman cheated you, did he?" Stoddard grinned drunkenly.

Isaac Banyon's face reddened and, rattler-quick, he leapt the distance to the table. With a sweeping motion he slung Stoddard's drink in his face. "Don't ye be drinking a drop without my permission, and don't be thinking any heathen be man enough to cheat Captain Isaac Banyon."

Stoddard swayed and tottered slowly to his feet, his jaw set tight, drops of grog forming along its hard line. He didn't bother to wipe them away. "A man might cross me once too often," he muttered through clenched teeth.

"Then let this be the time." Banyon stepped even closer to the first mate. "I'll have no insubordination aboard my ship, and if you're not tucked into your bunk singing lullabies by the count of ten, I'll chuck your sogger hide overboard without your cut of the *mui gai* money, and ye can find a new berth."

The muscles in Stoddard's shoulders and arms knotted, but he made no move toward the big captain, nor even one to wipe the grog away as it formed another drop on the end of his nose.

Banyon held his gaze, steely-eyed, until Stoddard calmed down and looked away. Then the captain stepped aside and, fists balled at his sides, allowed Stoddard to pass. Banyon reached down and caught Vandersteldt by the collar. "And ye'll stand extra watch for a week, Dutchman."

"But Stoddard broke out the grog, sir."

"For a week, extra watch, starting now. Now get ye gear and get up and relieve the anchor watch."

Vandersteldt said nothing, just hurried out and headed for the fo'c'sle and his coat.

"It's a bloody shame you can't get decent sailing men," Abner grumbled. Banyon shot him a look that would curdle milk. "Would you like a cup of tea afore you turn in, Captain?" Abner asked quickly.

"I'd like one man aboard this vessel who does his task," Banyon snapped. His movements stiff, he left the room.

Abner listened to the captain stomp down the passageway and slam his door. He decided that he would have a cup of tea, laced with the grog left in Vandersteldt's cup. Since the captain had retired for the night, why let it go to waste? He smiled to himself. A man needs some comfort after standing to Isaac Banyon's insults.

Clint shushed the Chinese fisherman with a finger to his lips as they neared the *Amnity,* and the man complied by barely moving his oar. Pointing to the forward anchor rode, Clint leaned far out and caught it. He steadied the boat under the rode, passed the fisherman a gold piece, shoved his Colt's rifle deep into his belt at the back of his pants, and began a hand-over-hand climb up the rode. He reached the chain scupper, managed to get a foot in the opening, and stood high enough that he could see over the rail. There was no sound on the forward deck, only the quiet singing of a sailor, his tenor voice relishing a trip back to O' Virginny, in the fo'c'sle below. Clint leapt up over the rail and waved to Gideon, who followed his example up the rode. In a second they stood side by side, watching the Chinese scull away.

"There should be a man standing anchor watch aft," Clint whispered. "The Chinese who's supposed to help us will be in the fo'c'sle, unless he's on watch."

"So do we check aft, or the fo'c'sle?"

"Aft. Someone's still awake forward."

Clint crept along the rail in the darkness, his long time at sea a godsend as he wove through the fixed gear, ventilators, and lines on the foredeck. Gideon stumbled along behind, as out of place as a feathered and fluffed whore in a Sunday service.

Clint moved across the main deck and crouched behind a six-pound waist cannon, then again at the raised quarterdeck. The man standing anchor watch sat on a ventilator, quietly enjoying the calm sea, smoking.

"Can't tell if he's Chinese in the dim light," Clint whispered when Gideon joined him in a crouch.

"Then let's walk up and find out," Gideon said, standing upright.

"I'll go first. There may not be any dark-skinned men aboard. Chances are he'll mistake me for one of the crew."

Gideon waved him on. Clint climbed the short ladder, leaned his rifle against a scuttlebutt, and shoved his revolver and holster around behind his hip so they were hidden. He moved aft with the rolling gait of a sailor.

"A quiet night for it," Clint called out. He was not a Chinese, Clint decided as the man looked up. The anchor watch, a swarthy dark-skinned Portuguese, glanced at his visitor with little concern, then looked out over the sea and took a deep draw on his pipe.

He expelled a roiling puff of smoke. "Near the last of the quiet nights, I suspect. We'll be well west of the Farallons in blue water by this time tomorrow." He glanced back at Clint. "You just sign on?"

Before Clint could answer, Gideon, who had approached the man from the other side of the mizzenmast, raised his belt gun and slapped it across the man's temple. The pipe flew, showering dottle and sparks across the holystoned deck. The man sagged without a moan or kick.

"He wasn't a Chinaman," Gideon commented, staring down at the fallen anchor watch.

Clint smiled at his friend's cold efficiency. "Tomorrow his aching head will wish he had been," Clint said, then grabbed the tail of a halyard and began binding the man. Gideon helped Clint back him up against the mizzenmast, and they tied him in a sitting position. Gideon tore away a long piece of the man's shirttail and gagged him.

Clint turned down the hanging anchor lantern so it would cast even less light across the deck, then started around to the entrance to the fo'c'sle. The singing had stopped and no light escaped from the fo'c'sle hatch.

Clint reached for the latch just as the door jerked open.

"Who the hell are you?" a ruddy-faced man asked. He was only one man, but twenty-eight sleeping men lay behind him.

CHAPTER TWENTY-THREE

Apolonia hesitated outside the cover to the hold where Gaspar and the men were imprisoned. She wondered where in the world she could possibly find a tool such as Gaspar wanted. The ship was a maze of rooms and storage areas and chests. She could search for a month if she wasn't lucky — and if she didn't get caught.

She slowly started up the ladder. She felt like a small rabbit coming out of its hole to face a pack of dogs. When her head cleared the deck above, she hesitated and listened. The light was still on in the cabin where she had heard men earlier, but it was silent now. She had not searched the small empty cabin nearest the ladder. Maybe she could find a tool there.

She moved to the door and found the cold brass handle. A tremor raced up her backbone, cautioning her — but she didn't heed it. She conquered it and ever so slowly worked the latch. The door swung wide and she stepped in.

A ham-sized hand snaked out of the darkness and closed over her throat. She felt herself being lifted off the deck and plunged into a narrow bunk, where she could barely move. She tried to scream, but the hand clasped so tightly she was afraid she would suffocate.

She tried to kick, but the man smothered her with his body, forcing himself between her legs.

"Polly, my little Mexican lass," the gruff voice said, "don't you be fightin', now. If you scream or say a word, the captain'll know ye are sneaking about the boat, and he'll chain ye in the hold for the rats to nibble on."

Fear numbed her limbs. But the thought of even that fate was not as terrible as what was happening to her. Stoddard's hand found its way along her leg and under her smock. She tried to get a knee between his, but his hold tightened even more.

She was afraid she would pass out. Even if she were unconscious, she knew this brute of a man would have his way with her. As fear flooded her, the bile rose in her throat, and her heart hammered in fear.

Clint stared at the square-jawed ruddy-faced sailor who blocked his way into the fo'c'sle.

"Who the hell am I?" Clint repeated, stalling for time. "Who the hell am I?" he said, this time in indignation. "I'm the by-God San Francisco harbor commissioner, that's who the hell I am! What the hell is this ship doing anchored in an unauthorized area? And who the hell are you?"

"Vandersteldt . . . second mate," he mumbled, a puzzled look on his face. He stepped out of the fo'c'sle and turned to pull the door closed. Gideon didn't wait. This time he brought a belaying pin across the man's head. The crunch made Clint wince.

The Dutchman fell like a timber, the thump echoing across the silent deck.

Clint stepped back so he could get a good swing with the butt of his Colt's at anyone who came out of the fo'c'sle to see what the commotion was. But it was unnecessary. No sounds came from inside. He motioned for Gideon to tie the ruddy-faced man up and, as he set about the task, Clint slipped inside the crew's quarters.

He found a candle where one always rested on shipboard — in a sconce mounted on the base of the foremast where it passed through the fo'c'sle — and lit it. His muscles bunched when the lucifer flared, but no one moved.

The quiet coughing and snoring of sleeping men were the only sounds in the low-ceiling, three-cornered room.

Knowing the pecking order of ships, Clint quickly made his way to the most forward bunks, the smallest and tightest of those in the fo'c'sle. Odds were, a Chinese on board would not have his pick of the better locations.

In the last bunk forward, he spied an Oriental face. Quickly checking the other forward bunks to make sure there was not more than one, Clint clamped his hand firmly over the man's mouth. Willie's eyes snapped open, wide with fear. Clint bent low and whispered, "Zhang Ho sent me, Willie." Willie's eyes signaled recognition of the name.

Slowly Clint released the little man, who quietly moved his covers aside. Willie found the pair of trousers rolled up at the foot of his bunk and pulled them on under his nightshirt.

Clint headed out and Willie followed without bothering to pull on his boots.

They reached the deck and Clint extended his hand. As Willie Boy shook, he glanced down at the fallen, now-bound second mate, then craned his neck to locate the anchor watch.

"He's tied up too," Clint offered.

Gideon stepped forward. "Where are the women?"

"They aft, below officers' mess, in passenger quarters."

"Locked in?" Clint asked.

Without answering, Willie Boy dug in his trousers pocket and produced a key with a satisfied smile.

Clint snatched it out of his hand. "You lower the captain's boat for us, then go back to your bunk." Willie nodded his head and smiled gratefully — his participation was to be over quickly. He hurried aft to the quarterdeck to lower the tender. Clint and Gideon followed, but then headed to the hatchway below.

They checked their weapons at the hatch, then quietly descended the half ladder. Clint motioned to Gideon, making sure he saw the light coming from the officers' mess just as Gideon caught a muffled sound from the closest door off the passageway.

The quiet cry was little more than a gurgled moan, but it sounded panicked and female. Gideon put his ear to the door and heard another keening whimper, followed by a choking sob. It steeled his resolve.

He cocked a foot and kicked the door so hard it flew off its hinges and slammed against the bulkhead across the little cabin. Storming in, he caught the white reflection of Stoddard's buttocks, his belted pants being shoved below them with a gnarled hand.

In a step, Gideon's booted foot found the target and he kicked, propelling Stoddard forward. The man's face crashed into the bulkhead at the end of the bunk.

A muffled scream from the girl who still lay pinned below Stoddard angered Gideon even more, but the man spun out of the bunk and sprang to his feet before Gideon had a chance to kick him again.

Stoddard, his pants at his knees, feigned a punch, then ducked and dove across the room, burying his burly head in Gideon's midsection. Clint tried to get into the room, but Gideon's body crashed out into the passageway. Stoddard followed, bellowing and clawing to pull on his trousers.

Clint sidestepped. Stoddard leapt on Gideon, who had backstepped a foot into the ladder well and fallen. His massive attacker pummeled his face.

Clint could not get a clear swing at the first mate's head, for the fighting men rolled under the half ladder. Instead he slammed the Colt's butt into Stoddard's ribs again and again, beating the breath from him and dislodging him from atop Gideon.

Apolonia suddenly appeared in the doorway, her face ashen.

"We're from your father!" Clint said quickly, recognizing her from her picture. Before she could respond, Stoddard knocked her back into the cabin in an effort to get to his feet. He spun to face Clint in a half crouch, but a well-placed kick from Gideon sent him sprawling back into the cabin after Apolonia.

In a bounce the man reappeared, a half scowl, half grin on his face — and an ugly long-bladed knife in his hand. This time Clint had a clear swing and the butt of the Colt's crunched into the side of his head. The big man merely bounced against the bulkhead and glared, if a bit cockeyed, at Clint. The butt of the Colt's slammed into the man again, this time splattering his nose across his face, blood across the bulkhead, and dropping him.

Stoddard collapsed heavily on his back across the ladder well to the deck below. A well-placed stomp from Gideon, who had regained his feet, and Stoddard folded and clattered down the ladder.

Apolonia made her way back into the doorway. Clint reached for her, but she screamed and pointed over his shoulder.

Gideon charged past Clint in the narrow passageway, knocking him aside and sending his rifle spinning down the hall. Gideon met the bellowing charge of the captain head-on. The clash straightened both of them, and the blast of a pistol filled the narrow way with flame and acrid smoke. Gideon reeled away.

Clint dove into Isaac Banyon, driving him back into his cabin. The reflection on the gun barrel in the captain's hand brought a rush to Clint, and he pummeled the man's face with both fists, snapping his head back, forcing him deeper into the room.

Banyon tried to raise his pistol, but Clint found the barrel and they struggled.

Fighting chest to chest, they seemed stalemated. Then the captain grimaced over his full beard and ever so slowly the barrel inched up.

Like a wildcat protecting a den of kittens, Apolonia Vega raced across the room and drove the sharp metal points of the dividers deep into the captain's shoulder. He growled and his eyes filled with pain, but still he managed to lift the muzzle another few inches. Apolonia uttered a primal snarl, jerked the dividers out, and struck again and again with the needle-sharp ends.

The pistol clattered to the floor and Banyon clawed at his injured shoulder and collapsed. Clint kicked the pistol away, grabbed Apolonia's arm, and guided her out of the room.

Gideon stood in the passageway, his face slack, one arm hanging limply, dripping blood. Realizing his friend had taken the captain's bullet, Clint shouted at him, "Can you make it up the ladder?"

"I think so." Gideon turned to the ladder. Clint gave him a shove up behind Apolonia. They hesitated on the deck.

"What about the other women, and Gaspar?" Apolonia asked. When Clint did not answer, she tried to run back into the hatch. Clint caught her waist with his hands and picked her up. He hauled her, kicking and screaming, to the rail and dropped her over. *That Chinaman had better have done what I told him to do,* Clint thought as he turned to help Gideon, but his friend was already on the rail. He jumped and Clint followed.

Clint dove, plunging deep into the murky water, and surfaced to the sound of a choking and spitting Apolonia Vega.

"I . . . can't . . . swim," she sputtered between gags.

His eyes searched the ship's waterline and, proof of Willie's loyalty, Clint saw the captain's boat bobbing where Willie had lowered it. Clint swam to the girl, gathered the back of her smock in a hand, and dragged her to the boat. As soon as she had a hold on its gunwales, he turned back to try to find Gideon.

He was nowhere to be seen.

CHAPTER TWENTY-FOUR

Four white devil guards made it out of the Barracoon with two sacks full of gold. Their waiting horses took them south, the only way other than the sea that they could get out of San Francisco.

As soon as Zhang Ho's guards had discovered their route of escape, he and his guards boarded the *Fei Dao,* a slender sailing sloop with eight oars whose name meant "Swift Knife." Properly manned, she was the fastest boat in the harbor. With the wind at their back and the help of the powerful guards who served as oarsmen, she averaged fourteen knots on her trip down the bay.

She passed the new mooring place of the *Amnity* well before Clint and Gideon arrived, and reached Palo Alto, a place the Mexicans had named for its tall timber. Ho and the guards disembarked and by midnight had made their way inland to wait in the trees, and the darkness, along the roadside. Their patience was rewarded when the white guards, still wearing their Barracoon arm bands, galloped into the waiting hatchets of the Celestials. The white guards were taken by complete surprise. The battle lasted only seconds.

The horses were set free, the arm bands stripped away so the bodies would have no connection with the Barracoon, and the dead guards were dragged into the brush and left stripped and unburied for the coyotes, crows, and gulls.

Even though he sailed against the wind, taking much more time, the trip home was a joy to Zhang Ho — he was content.

With rapid strokes Clint swam to the spot where Gideon had hit the water. Taking a deep breath, he dove and stroked down, down until his hands hit the muddy bottom. He searched frantically, but found nothing. His lungs crying for relief, he kicked off the bottom and shot to the surface, finding himself alongside the hull. The tide was coming in and the current increasing. He heard a slapping sound, then a cough in the darkness, and followed it.

Gideon, too, was alongside the *Amnity,* desperately clinging, trying to find a handhold on her slimy barnacled side.

Clint grabbed Gideon's collar from behind and kicked off the ship's rough side. "Kick your feet . . . don't move your arms."

"Can't move one," Gideon confided calmly.

Gideon's upper body went limp in Clint's grasp, but his legs took up a rhythmic kicking. By the time they reached the side of the captain's shore boat, Apolonia had managed to get her upper body over the gunwales. Gideon grasped the boat and Clint put a hand under Apolonia's bottom and shoved. She flew into the boat.

"Unhook the lines," Clint instructed her, glancing up at the *Amnity*'s rail, fearing disaster. He moved to boost Gideon. Apolonia, completing the task of casting off the block and tackle, helped the big black man aboard, then collapsed in exhaustion. Clint hoisted himself into the rocking boat, positioned himself on the rowing thwart, fixed the oars in the oarlocks, and pulled for the shore.

"There! There they be!" he heard a shout ring from the deck of the *Amnity*. He pulled oar as he never had.

Luckily a low haze lay over the water and the sliver of a moon offered little light.

"Get down," Clint cautioned as the boat cut through the water. Almost before he finished,

284

a lead ball cut the air with a deadly whistle across the bow of the little boat and he saw the flash of a musket at the taffrail of the ship.

"Bloodly hell," Clint swore, realizing he had left the rifle behind on the ship. That rifle meant a lot to him.

Behind them the ominous silhouettes at the rail faded out of sight in the fog, and Clint slowed his pace. They would make it.

Two more wild shots hummed a frustrated note nearby after Clint worked the left oar and changed his path of flight.

"See if you can stop his bleeding," Clint instructed Apolonia, who carefully tore away the ragged bloodstained shirt at Gideon's left shoulder.

She checked the wound carefully, then began to tear away the hem of her smock. "This will hurt," she said. Without hesitation and with deft hands, she packed the gaping hole.

"You're right," Gideon calmly agreed. "It hurts. But thank you." He glanced up at Clint. "Will they follow?"

"I'm sure they're launching the longboat now. But they'll never catch up."

"My friends are aboard that ship," Apolonia said.

"More Californio women?" Clint asked between strokes with the oars.

"Five other señoritas and Gaspar Cota and three of his vaqueros."

"I'm sorry we can't help," Clint said, his tone cold, his mind on the Kaweah ranch. "But my job was to get you home safely. We'll report the other women, and maybe, with your testimony, the authorities will do something about them. As far as I'm concerned, Gaspar can shovel his own stall."

Apolonia fell suddenly silent, but she looked in the direction of the ship until the little boat grounded against the mud flat.

The horses were tied and waiting where Gideon had left them. Clint mounted Diablo, swinging up behind Apolonia, and they were off well before the crew of the *Amnity* was able to get the longboat ashore. Clint had to stop and tie Gideon to the saddle before they got back to Hardy's. Apolonia stayed with Gideon while Clint fetched a doctor, who arrived quickly to tend Gideon's wound.

"Through and through," Doc Baxter said as he dressed the wound in Gideon's shoulder. "But he's lucky. It missed the bone. The bleeding has almost stopped and I won't have to cauterize it. Rest and care and good food is the order of the day." The doctor led Clint outside. "If it goes green, call me and I'll load him up with laudanum and cut away the bad flesh."

"Thank you." Clint paid Baxter with one of the few gold coins he had left. "Stay with him," Clint instructed Apolonia, "while I fetch him a nurse."

Clint trotted the two blocks and entered the El Dorado. Pushing his way through the crowd, while Sultry was singing, he made his way to her rooms to get Su Chin. Then they exited through the alley door. Impatient with her hobble, Clint carried her back to the livery and deposited her in Gideon's room.

Then he returned to the El Dorado with Apolonia in tow and entered via the alley. They were waiting when Sultry returned from the stage.

"Where's Su Chin?" Sultry asked as she swished into the room. She sat at her dressing table and, in the mirror, noticed the beautiful Californio girl on the settee. She began to re-move her heavy makeup without greeting the señorita.

Clint cleared his throat. "This is Apolonia Vega. With your permission, your new guest. Gideon took a ball through the shoulder and is flat on his back. I took Su Chin to Hardy's to nurse him."

Sultry spun on her stool to face Clint. "Is he all right?"

"He'll be all right, with rest and barring any infection."

She looked Apolonia up and down. "I swear, Clint Ryan, the Mexicans gave you the right handle. You lasso these women in like a Texican after longhorns."

"Then she can stay? It's just until tomorrow. I promised her a visit to the marshal's office before I take her home. And I sure as hell can't have her stay with me. Her father might not think that's rescuin'."

"Then when you get the señorita home, your job is finished and you can head for the gold country?"

"I never said I'd take your nursemaid job."

"But you're about to." She flashed him a smug smile. "After all, fair is fair. You haven't had any compunction about asking me to take *your* nursemaid jobs."

He looked around in frustration. "After I get her home, I'll have a herd of horses to drive south." But if Apolonia didn't have a safe place to stay he might not have a herd of horses to worry about, and with Jasper and the bevy of bartenders acting like Sultry was their chaste younger sister, backstage at the El Dorado was the safest place he knew of. And as Sultry pointed out, fair was fair.

Besides, he was bone-aching tired and needed the rest and didn't have the energy to argue.

Sultry fluttered her eyes at him. "The new

288

fields at Sonoma are south of here, like this ranch you talk about. You can drive your herd as far as there. I'll begin and end my tour there, then you can pick them up again when I've finished and drive them to hell, for all I care." *By that time,* she vowed, *you won't want to leave me for ten thousand horses.*

"Twenty dollars a day and found against ten percent of your take," Clint said, knowing that that would bust the deal.

"And Gideon will go along?"

"I can't speak for Gideon," Clint said, wondering if his alligator mouth had overloaded his hummingbird backside.

"Done." Sultry rose, her look triumphant, and extended her hand.

"Done," Clint said quietly. With reluctance and a deep sigh, he accepted her soft handshake. She had roped him in and hog-tied him with far more skill than the Texicans she spoke about.

Clint sat down on the settee beside Apolonia and took her hand in his. "I'll see you at daybreak."

Sparks flew from Sultry's eyes, but she didn't say what she was thinking. Instead she instructed, "Don't wake me at that obscene time of day."

"No, ma'am," Clint said, and headed for the door. "Or should I say, no, boss man?"

"Only if you want to join Gideon in the recovery bed." She shot Clint a killing glance and a smile as thin as the fingernail she had begun to file.

Clint hurried back to Hardy's to check on Gideon once more. Content that Su Chin was watching him with studied care, he fell into his own narrow bed.

He was asleep in half a heartbeat, but he tossed and turned. The thought of the other Californio girls at the mercy of Harlan Stoddard and Isaac Banyon gnawed at him like a starving dog on a new bone.

If he saved him from a few months in the yardarms, he might even get to see Gaspar Cota's flapping jaw shut for more than a second.

But he doubted it.

CHAPTER TWENTY-FIVE

Apolonia was beautiful, wearing one of Sultry's most conservative dresses. Still the sleek black gown showed off Apolonia's ripe figure as if she, too, were a showgirl. She and Clint stood in Portsmouth Square, near the squat Mission Delores in the oldest part of the city, and awaited the arrival of Marshal Larson at his office. Clint had thought long and hard about risking a visit to the marshal's office — but Thad McPherson was dead, and he had said he had not had a chance to talk to Larson about "John Ryan."

They saw Larson at the end of the block and waited patiently as he glad-handed each of the merchants between there and his office.

"Well, howdy there," he said, exhibiting his politician's smile and snatching off his hat with his left hand while extending his right to Clint. It wasn't the kind of greeting a man with a warrant for your arrest would extend. With new confidence, Clint launched into the reason for his visit.

"Marshal, this is Apolonia Vega, the girl I was telling you about."

The marshal nodded. He opened his door and stepped aside, ushering Clint and Apolonia ahead of him.

"I'm glad you showed up, Ryan. Saves me from having to come and find you. I need a statement from you and from that darkie friend of yours about that shindig at the Barracoon." His brows furrowed like a peach pit. "Folks don't much cater to a Negra being involved in a shootin'."

He politely pulled a chair in front of his broad oak desk and seated Apolonia, then took his own chair as Clint dragged one up.

Marshal Larson snaked a cigar out of the desk drawer, leaned back and lit up, and put a foot up while he enjoyed the first draw. He exhaled a cloud of smoke.

"I see she's all right, just as I suspected." He wore a smug look and laughed gruffly. "Run off with one of those fancy-dan Mexican lads —" He frowned at Apolonia. "Having a little jollification, were you, girl?"

"No," Apolonia said coldly. "I was taken prisoner."

"Taken prisoner!" Larson repeated, his

voice laced with skepticism.

"Taken prisoner," Clint snapped. "Gideon LaMont and I boarded the *Amnity* last night and found her here."

"Boarded? Without Captain Banyon's permission? It's a wonder you aren't hanging from his yardarm right now." He turned to Apolonia. "Captain Banyon is a well-respected man. This sounds a little farfetched. Were you locked up or chained?" Larson asked.

"She wasn't at the time. She was being accosted —" Clint glanced at her, concerned that she would be embarrassed, but her look remained hard and intense, "by the first mate, Stoddard, in his cabin."

"Sometimes," Larson said with a snicker, "with these dark-skinned girls, it's hard to tell bein' accosted from bein' pleasured." A slow smile crept across Larson's mouth. "Are you sure you didn't like that, girly?"

Clint was on his feet before Larson finished his insulting question. He leaned forward, both hands on Larson's desk.

"You know, Larson, you're as insulting as you are ignorant." Larson jumped to his feet also, but Clint continued. "I've brought you proof that the *Amnity* and her captain are behind these abductions, and all you want to do is insult this girl who's spent a week locked up on a slave ship that masquerades as a freighter. Are you going to go down there and get the other girls off her or not?"

Larson's face was as red as Apolonia's lips. "Down where?" he snapped, gnawing on his cigar.

"Hunter's Point," Clint fired back.

The marshal's side door opened, and one of Larson's deputies looked in, wondering what the raised voices were all about. Larson relaxed back in his chair and plopped his feet back up on the desk.

"I'm going to overlook your crack about ignorant, Ryan, 'cause my jail is full up from last night. As for insulting . . . these so-called Californios bring the insults on themselves." A wry smile crossed his face. "Besides, Hunter's Point is also out of my jurisdiction."

Clint's fists balled at his sides, but he could do little good for the girls still on board the *Amnity* if he was cooling his heels in Larson's filthy jail.

Without speaking, he spun on his heel and led Apolonia out of the office.

"You get back here afore the week's out and give me a statement about that mess at the Barracoon," Larson called after him, but the slamming door shut him off.

"What are we going to do?" Apolonia asked, trotting along to keep pace with his brisk stride.

"You're going to go back to Sultry's and stay out of sight. I'm going to get some help and resolve your problem."

"My problem?"

"Those other girls and Gaspar Cota are sure as hell not my problem," he snapped. Then his scowl faded. "Pardon my French."

"French?" she asked.

"Just a figure of speech. Hurry up!"

She trotted along beside him, sleek and beautiful, as he headed back to the El Dorado.

While Clint had been arguing with Larson, Isaac Banyon, Harlan Stoddard, and ten of the crew of the *Amnity* arrived at the Barracoon, all armed with muskets, sidearms, and blades. Zhang Ho and his guards were not back from chasing the thieves.

Banyon, his arm and shoulder bandaged and in a sling from Apolonia's well-placed strokes with the dividers, roared at the little Chinese man who served as the Barracoon's swamper and watchman, and who had just told him about the robbery.

"By the devil's eyes, I'll draw and quarter the heathen bastard and feed his offal to the hogs, and ye, too, if ye lie to me."

"I told you," — the little man quaked — "honorable Ho seeks men who robbed gold. He said you wait here. He has your share."

With his good right arm, Banyon snatched the man up by the front of his robe, lifting him clear off the floor. "And I'm to cool my heels here while he gets farther and farther away? The hell I will. How did the yellow scum go? By land or sea?"

"By sea, on the boat *Fei Dao.*"

Banyon stormed outside and reboarded the wagon he had rented from the Chinese fishing village. Harlan Stoddard, his nose grotesquely swollen and his eyes raccoon black, whipped up the broken-down horse and they lumbered off toward the wharves.

With Apolonia back safe at the El Dorado, Clint was on his way to the wharves also. Mounted on Diablo, he reined up and watched Banyon's wagon approach. Clint hoisted his Colt's revolver an inch, just to make sure it rode free and easy in its holster, and locked eyes with Stoddard, then Banyon, who also rode in the driver's seat. Stoddard pulled rein.

Clint spoke quietly. "You've got more Californio ladies aboard that scow of yours, Banyon. You'll not get out of the harbor with them."

"I should shoot you down right here," Banyon roared, and the sailors in the rear of the wagon started to bring their weapons up.

Leather whispered, and Clint held the

296

cocked Colt's in hand, its deadly eye staring at the surprised sea captain.

"Any man who cocks one of those old pieces of junk will wear this bastard's brains."

Not a man twitched.

Banyon's eyes never left the end of the Colt's muzzle, which was not three feet from his face. "Whip up this wagon, Stoddard," Banyon commanded coldly.

Carefully Harlan tapped the old mare's flank with the buggy whip, and the horse began to clomp away. The Colt's tracked the wagon as it rolled by, and none of the men in the back took their eyes off it or moved.

"I'll see you long before you pass through the Golden Gate," Clint called after them.

"I'll rein up as soon as we get out of pistol range and shoot that son of a bitch with his own rifle," Stoddard offered quietly, toeing Clint's Colt's rifle, which rode in the floorboards under Stoddard's feet, stained across the butt with Stoddard's own blood.

"Not here, but you may get your chance," Banyon growled. "He's a brazen bastard, and I expect he'll do just as he says."

"Let him come," Stoddard wheezed, for he couldn't breathe through his swollen nose. "I'll be ready for him this time."

"That would be a pleasant change, Mr. Stoddard." Banyon glanced at his first mate and shook his head in disgust. "But far more important than Clint Ryan and your pride is Zhang Ho and my money. We'll check the waterfront, and if we don't spot the *Fei Dao*, I must presume he's run for it. The *Amnity* will chase that sloop and the yellow scum down, and I'll see him swinging at the end of my halyards.

"Hurry this nag up," Banyon snapped.

Clint needed help, and it was now plain that he wasn't going to get any from the law.

But he thought he knew where he might buy some loyalty, even if only for a short time. Even if he would have to watch his back.

For over an hour he searched the Barbary Coast, looking for the guns he needed, before he reined Diablo up in front of the Outback Roo. He dismounted and tied the big palomino where he could watch it from inside the bat-wing doors, and entered. As he had hoped, he spotted Fish Shaddock and his big friend, Booker Whittle, standing at the bar among another half dozen Sydney Ducks.

Clint boldly pushed his way through the men, faced Fish, and got right to the point. "I need to hire you men for a day's honest work."

Most of them looked at him like he'd lost his mind, but Fish immediately responded. "I act as the agent here, mate. You talk with me if you want help from the Ducks."

"Yeah," Booker agreed. His scarred face broke with a snaggletoothed grin. "Fish is boss."

"Come over to my office," Fish said, motioning Clint to a table. Booker loitered nearby, but stayed just out of earshot.

"What's the work?" Fish asked.

"Pistol and rifle work. Settin' some conscripts loose from the *Amnity*."

Fish laughed and slapped his thigh. "That's a by-Christ lark. We'll be gettin' paid comin' and goin'." His laugh faded. "What's the pay, mate?"

"Twenty dollars a man for the try, win or lose, and twenty dollars a head bonus for every conscript freed."

"How many?"

"Nine, by my count."

"In gold?" Fish's voice dropped, and he bent closer.

"Gold," Clint assured him.

"You got that much gold on you now?" Fish asked, glancing at Booker.

"You might be crazy, Fish" — Clint smiled — "but don't take me for a fool."

"Then how do I know we get paid?"

Clint reached into his pocket and pulled his last five-dollar gold pieces out. He slapped them on the table. "This'll seal the bargain. You get the rest when the work's done."

Fish swiped the money off the table and pocketed it, then extended his slender hand, and they shook. Clint started to get up. "Wait," Fish said, and motioned him closer. "No need for the boys to know about the bonus. Let's keep that 'tween you and me," he said, his look hopeful and his tone conspiratorial.

"Just you and me, Fish," Clint assured him. He didn't give a damn how the money was split; he was more concerned with where he would get it and what these Ducks would do if he could not produce at the end of the day.

"Get your boys outside," Clint instructed. "And Fish — let them know that I'm running this operation. They take orders from me."

"Your gold, your orders," Fish agreed, then moved away to the bar to strike his own bargain with the Ducks.

CHAPTER TWENTY-SIX

Clint mounted Diablo and wondered how he was going to get eight men back to the *Amnity*. He had no money left and he sure as hell couldn't give the Ducks even a hint of that fact. He glanced to where they stood on the boardwalk, awaiting his orders.

Hardy would give him credit for horses for the day, he thought. Then he looked out on the wharf and saw Zhang Ho and the guards disembarking the *Fei Dao*.

Maybe things are going my way, he decided, and called to Fish, "I'll be right back."

Spurring Diablo, he galloped through the piles of goods, Diablo's pounding hooves making a hollow drumming ring on the wooden planks, out to where the little sloop had tied up alongside Long Wharf.

Pulling rein, Clint dismounted before Diablo came to a complete stop. The guards surrounded Zhang Ho protectively, but relaxed when they saw who the rider was.

"Ho, I need your help to get those girls off the *Amnity* before she sails. Do this for me and I'll help you recover the money the guards stole."

"That problem is resolved, honorable friend. I can offer money, I can offer men if I have time to hire those who Banyon cannot identify with the Barracoon or the tong, but as I told you, I cannot be tied to the effort."

"Have you given Banyon his cut yet?"

"No. I expect he'll be waiting at the Barracoon."

"Banyon was heading away from the Barracoon the last time I saw him, looking mad as a stepped-on rattler and twice as nasty. But I hope he is going back there to wait for you." *That'll mean fewer men to face aboard the Amnity,* Clint thought. "Money I'll need," he told Ho, "and that boat."

"You can sail her?"

"Like I built her," Clint said.

Ho thoughtfully stroked the tails of his long mustache, then smiled. "If it comes to it, I will say you have stolen her."

"That'll work," Clint agreed. He called down the wharf and waved to his new gang of Ducks. Tying Diablo's reins to the saddle horn, he slapped him on the rump and sent him running, knowing he would go straight back to the livery and that Hardy would care for him.

"May your ancestors remember you fondly," Zhang Ho said, then hurried his men away, including the one who served as captain of the *Fei Dao.*

By the time the Ducks got alongside, the jib was tied off and Clint was running up the main sail of the sloop. He waved them down and they took up positions at the oar thwarts.

"I get seasick," Fish said sheepishly, "and these boys ain't partial to rowing."

"God willing, the wind'll do the work," Clint said just as the sail billowed and he cast off the dock line. He took the tiller and swung the quick little sloop away from the wharf.

"Maybe the work, but how about me belly?"

They had been under way for almost two hours when they made out the *Amnity* under full sail and heading northerly, the direction of the Golden Gate and open sea. She heeled in the brisk wind less than two miles away from them, on a diagonal course — a course Clint did not believe he could intercept.

"Damn," Clint grumbled under his breath. Fish looked up from the bottom of the *Fei Dao,* where he'd been since he'd finished chumming with the contents of his stomach.

"What?" Fish asked, moaning quietly.

"The *Amnity*. She's under full sail and heading for the China Sea."

"We still get the money. Win or lose, you said."

"With a little luck, I can cut across her bow." Clint spoke more to himself than to the Ducks, but as soon as he adjusted the sloop's course and trimmed her sails, the *Amnity* pointed even closer to the wind as if she were attempting to bear down on the sloop.

Clint quickly made a mental note of the armaments on board the packet ship. She was no cruiser, but he remembered a small six-pound waist gun amidships on each side, and an even smaller three-pound swivel gun mounted on her aft rail.

The sloop, too, was armed. A little two-pound swivel gun rested on her bow.

"Do you know how to load that gun?" Clint called to Booker, who sat at a forward thwart.

Booker examined the two-foot iron cannon with slow but studied thoroughness. "Can't be much of a chore," he finally said.

The bow of the sloop was decked-over three feet back. Booker searched under the cover and came up with a two-inch-bore cannon and a small keg of powder.

"Don't bother with the ball. Load her with five ounces of powder and two dozen pistol balls." Booker looked at Clint for a moment, studying the suggestion. "We can't do a damn bit of harm to the hull," Clint ordered. "It's the men we're after."

Booker nodded, and set about the task as the *Amnity* closed to within half a mile.

He rammed the small swabber home, ready to fire, but the *Amnity* swung away, her course perpendicular to the *Fei Dao*. "Damn," Clint cursed under his breath, thinking that she was tacking, running for the open sea. But suddenly the sailors in her shrouds began to gather sail when she luffed in the turn, and she slowed.

"I'll be . . . she's heaving to —" before he finished, the six-pounder on her starboard amidships spat a bellow of fire and smoke.

"Duck!" Clint yelled, but rather than hitting the deck, each of the Sydney Ducks turned to see who Clint was yelling at.

Two of the men on the second thwart were blown overboard and the mainsail was holed as some of the grapeshot found its target.

"Jesus!" Booker yelled. Wide-eyed, he swung the bow gun on target. Leaning far back, he snatched a cigar out of the hand of the Duck who sat on the thwart behind him, puffed it with a long draw, and held it to the cannon's touch hole.

The sloop rattled with the recoil of the

swivel gun and Clint got a moment's satisfaction when the men amidships on board the *Amnity* dove for cover. But the little gun only bought he and his men a moment.

One more shot from the six-pounder and the *Fei Dao* would be out of business. He swung the tiller and headed the sloop for the bowsprit of the ship, where a webbing of line formed a net of last resort for any man who tumbled overboard, and where a bowsprit stay ran from the end low to the hull. Either of those could be handholds, and a path to the deck.

"She'll crush us," Booker warned.

Fish raised his head just over the gunwale, looking even sicker. He buried his face in his hands and hugged the bottom of the sloop.

"No, she won't," Clint said. "Get ready to jump for those lines. We'll climb up onto the bow!"

The Ducks stared at him as if he'd completely lost his mind.

Clint slid his Colt's from its holster. "Any man who doesn't make the jump will face the six-pounder on her far side, and that shot will be point-blank."

He didn't have to say any more as the men fixed their eyes on the bow of the *Amnity*, closing less than thirty yards ahead. Clint took a turn about the tiller with a dock line and fixed her course. Then he scrambled forward. Passing the mast, he threw the halyards off their cleats and the sails dropped, slowing the vessel.

At the last moment, Clint snatched up the keg of powder and tucked it under his arm. Only four of them made the jump. Two others fell back onto the *Fei Dao,* and one fell into the water. Fish didn't make the attempt, he was so sick. He elected to take his chances against the larboard six-pounder. The bow of the ship caught the aft of the sloop. With a sickening scrape, the sloop slammed against the hull of the ship and slid alongside, undamaged, but so close the starboard gunners had no shot.

The four from the *Fei Dao* made the deck, hidden by the three slack jib sails forward of the mizzenmast. They moved forward, seen only by the ship's crewmen high above tending the shrouds, and none of those men were armed. A man yelled a warning to the deck crew, who had gathered at the larboard rail, hoping to see the sloop destroyed by the six-pounder. Eight men, Banyon and Stoddard among them, looked overboard at the sloop scraping alongside the *Amnity.*

Clint, Booker, and the other two Ducks began a barrage of fire into the men.

Two men dropped immediately. Others

dove away in confusion. Banyon and Stoddard headed for the cover of the aft passageway, jumping down the half ladder.

"Booker, come with me!" Clint yelled. "You two keep those men in the shrouds. If a man from above tries to make the deck, shoot him. Keep those forward in the fo'c'sle."

The men above heard the order and headed up into the cover of the canvas and line.

Clint and Booker ran for the aft passageway. Two crewmen, one wounded, raised their hands in surrender.

"I want only Banyon and Stoddard," Clint yelled.

"They're all yours," one of the sailors told him.

A muzzle flashed in the darkness of the passageway, and Clint dove for the deck, the powder keg under one arm. The ball sliced his back, burning like a hot poker.

"Just a crease," Booker called from his position on the other side of the entrance.

Clint snapped off two shots into the darkness and heard a man scream. He rolled to the side and made the quarterdeck, out of sight of the passageway.

"I'm hit, Captain," he heard Stoddard shout.

"Stop ye whining, ye sogger," Banyon said. "Get up on deck and put the lead in that bastard Ryan."

"Get up there yourself!" Stoddard's voice had lost its power. Clint heard a cabin door slam, and he knew he had Banyon. Like a rat in a trap. He moved aft on the quarterdeck to a ventilator, studying it for a second. It looked big enough for what he had in mind. He went to the mizzenmast and jerked the anchor lantern down. With his belt knife he cut away a piece of line from a halyard, unraveled a third of it, and poured whale oil on it, soaking it.

He stuffed the homemade fuse into the bunghole of the gallon-sized powder keg and moved back to the ventilator.

"Do you have a lucifer?" he asked Booker, who stood forward, guarding the passageway from above.

Booker made his way aft to where Clint worked with the keg. "I believe I do," he said, a slow smile crossing his face.

Clint situated the keg in the ventilator. It would not drop all the way into the captain's cabin, for there were flutes to carry away seawater in case the deck was awash, but the opening it did have would be enough.

Clint dragged Booker's match across the bottom of the lantern, touched it to the fuse, and ran for the mizzenmast. Booker dove behind a deck box.

The blast rocked the ship and sent splinters

whistling across the deck and smoke and fire billowing up into the shrouds.

Clint rose, his ears ringing and his eyes watering from the noise and acrid smoke.

"That should do it," Clint said.

Booker gave him a wide snaggletoothed grin. "I believe that was one of the least neighborly things I ever saw done, mate."

"Let's go below and see if we did our task in a good and workmanlike manner." Clint jumped cautiously to the main deck and peered into the passageway. The door to the captain's cabin had been split in half and blown away.

"I'm hit already," Stoddard moaned from behind his closed door. "Please don't blow me up. I'm gut shot." His voice rang hollow with fear.

Clint palmed his Colt's and moved carefully past Stoddard's door to the rear, passing the door to the officers' mess. An Aston pistol lay on the floor. Stoddard's? Or Banyon's?

He stepped over half the door that blocked his way.

"Ye bastard!" The words came from behind him. The mess door crashed aside and powerful arms closed around his. "I'll kill ye with my own bare hands."

Clint tried to bring the pistol to bear, but Banyon, having shed the sling, held him in a crushing bear hug from behind.

"With my own hands," Banyon snarled. Clint could feel the man's beard on the side of his neck and smell his rancid breath. The ironlike arms forced Clint's ribs into his lungs.

"No, you won't." Booker's quiet voice wheezed through his many-times broken nose.

The roar of the pistol was so close to Clint's ear that its flame singed his hair. He dropped to the ground, but the captain fell on top of him. He turned to fight, his mind reeling from the shock of the blast, and kicked free. Glancing at Banyon, he realized half the man's head had been blown away.

"Jesus," Clint managed.

"You would have blown him all over the back of the ship," Booker said, umbrage on his scarred and bent face.

"True enough." Clint smiled and came to his feet. "True enough, indeed, mate. I thank you. At least I will when my ears stop ringing."

"Say nothing of it." Booker's twisted grin returned.

"Now, let's see to Mr. Stoddard and the ladies —"

"Ladies?" Booker's scarred eyebrows raised.

"Some of the conscripts are ladies, mate. But don't worry about it. You fellows will still

311

get your full share."

"I'll be damned," Booker mumbled.

"You get Stoddard's gun, and I'll get down below to free the women and their men. Then we'll get this scow back to San Francisco."

When Booker kicked open the first mate's door, Stoddard made no complaint. He never would again.

Clint smashed in the door to the passengers' cabin and found the women cowering together in a corner.

"You're free," he said simply.

"We were afraid that terrible explosion would sink the ship," Juanita Robles said. Then she realized what the man had said. "Free?"

"Free," he repeated. "Compliments of Don Carlos Vega."

The women crossed themselves, then sank to their knees to thank God and Don Carlos and the sandy-haired man who had kicked in their door.

It took Clint a while to locate Gaspar and the vaqueros, still chained and shackled in the hold.

He held a lantern in front of him and walked the ribs.

"You," Gaspar moaned. "You are the bastard behind this."

"Hardly, Cota. I'm the *gentleman* who's come to free you."

Gaspar glared in silence, reconciling in his mind that he was about to be freed by the Anglo. "You were paid well," Gaspar exclaimed with a haughty glance.

"You weren't part of the deal," Clint said.

"Don Cota," Chato snapped, "this man has been wounded trying to set us free."

Clint glanced down and saw the blood from the wound in his back had soaked his pants.

"You are a miserable whelp," Chato said, glaring at Gaspar, "and I will whip you one-handed if you don't tuck your flapping tongue back in your mouth — that is, if this gentleman will set us free." He glanced up at Clint. "I, for one, would be forever indebted if you would find a wrench and remove these cursed manacles."

"With pleasure," Clint said. "And you will be first, amigo."

Gaspar remained silent.

CHAPTER TWENTY-SEVEN

Clint made his peace with Sultry, telling her he would meet her and Jasper in Stockton in a week. From there, they would go on to Sonora together. He was surprised to learn when he returned to Hardy's that Su Chin had left Gideon in the care of a young Chinese man.

"Where'd she go, Gideon?" Clint asked his friend, who was sitting up, eating some Chinese vegetable concoction with enthusiasm.

"Don't know," he answered between bites. "She said this young man would lead me to her when I got well enough to worry about it."

"When do you think that's going to be?"

"Doc was here this morning. Said I could get up and around day after tomorrow."

"I've got to take Apolonia back to her father. I would have taken her today, but I had to make my peace with Marshal Larson and see to the *Amnity*. Seems Banyon has a wife who owns her now that he's met his maker. I've already sent word to Apolonia's father that she's all right, but I know he's anxious to have her home."

"I'd like to go along," Gideon said, "if you can wait until I can travel."

"I can wait, but I don't know if Sultry can stand Apolonia's company for that long. She looked at me like a bull at a bastard calf when I asked her if Apolonia could stay there awhile longer."

"Somehow," Gideon said with a knowing grin, "I think Sultry would keep a grizzly bear in her room if you asked."

"You've got more faith in my persuasive abilities than I have," Clint said with a laugh.

The next day Gideon convinced Clint that he could accompany him to find Su Chin. They took it slow and easy, and rested when Gideon began to tire. But they followed the Chinese boy down to the waterfront until he pointed ahead. "Su Chin house," he said, smiling proudly.

A long line of men, all shapes and sizes and colors, stretched for a block away from a small clapboard house.

"This Su Chin line," the boy said in his broken English.

Clint and Gideon looked at each other, each face reflecting the other's disappointment.

"I had hoped . . ." Clint started to say.

"Me too," Gideon agreed. "But I'll be damned if I'll wait in any consarned line when all I want to do is pay my respects."

They moved down the block, passing the group of men, and mounted the four steps in front of the house. The men in the front of the line gave them a hard look, but Gideon's sling and Clint's gift with the blarney got them by. "I'm with the city's new building and construction and pest inspection and —" Two massive guards met them in the tiny living room, making it clear that the two newcomers would wait their turn.

"Su Chin," Gideon shouted past the burly guards, who prepared to toss him and Clint out the door.

She hobbled to the kitchen door before the confrontation came to a head. "Wait, wait," she commanded the guards. "These are my partners."

She motioned the two of them in. Her dress was the finest green silk and she wore no jewelry, except a single red stone the size of Clint's thumb that hung at the end of a gold chain around her neck.

"Partner, hell," Clint grumbled. "I'm no purveyor of women."

"Come in, prease." She hobbled away.

Clint and Gideon moved around the guards,

giving them a conquering look. Su Chin reclined on a pillow on the kitchen floor. A griz-
zled full-bearded miner sat across from her
— sipping tea.

"You no mind, Mr. Johnston?" Su Chin
sweetly asked the man. "Only two more minutes. If you get back to end of line, I give
you ten minutes free next time."

"Surely, ma'am. Don't mind if I do." The
man scrambled to his feet and, hat in hand,
backed out of the kitchen. "I'll be back, as
soon as I get through the line again."

Clint's face still wore a look of disappointment, if a somewhat confused one. "What are
you doing, Su Chin?"

"Name now Ruby Su Chin," she answered,
looking a little embarrassed. "Su Chin work
to repay loan." She smiled demurely.

"Why do you call yourself Ruby?" Gideon
asked.

"First customer cheat Su Chin. Give me red
glass. Say is ruby." She blushed. "Su Chin
now have name to remind her not to be
cheated again."

"But you didn't have to . . . to . . ." Clint
wanted to tell her that an honest job would
have gotten the money back soon enough, but
he couldn't find just the right words.

"I think you no understan', honorable
Clint." She bowed, then giggled. "Miner pay

one ounce gold to have tea with Su Chin for ten minute . . . then maybe two ounce if Su Chin show honorable feet."

"Feet?" Gideon worked to keep his chin from dropping to his chest.

She turned and pulled a small box from under the pillow. Opening it, she offered it to Clint, who took it out of her hands. "Please to apply to loan," she said.

"There's over a hundred dollars in gold here," Clint stammered. "You couldn't have been at this for more than a day."

"Su Chin start ten o'clock this morning. Will have rest of money by end of week."

Gideon glanced at Clint. "We're in the wrong by-God business."

They visited awhile longer, taking up valuable time, until the clamor outside the door began to worry the guards.

Clint and Gideon rested on the top rail of Don Vega's corral fence, admiring the forty head of Andalusian horses — five stallions and thirty-five mares, some of them already with foal — that Clint and Sancho, the Vegas' head vaquero, had cut out of the huge herd that roamed the Rancho del Rio Ancho.

Apolonia Vega and her father stood a few steps away, arguing for the tenth time that morning.

"I'll not marry a man who's not of my choosing, Father."

"You'll do as I say," he snapped, his tone as adamant as hers.

"Never, never, never," she vowed. Tears forming in her eyes, she turned and ran for the hacienda.

"Women." Don Vega moaned. Walking over, he mounted the corral rail and sat next to Clint.

Apolonia stopped midway to the house. With a secret smile she turned and walked back to where her father, Clint, and Gideon sat.

"I cannot marry Gaspar Cota," Apolonia announced from behind the three men, who repositioned themselves on the rail to face her.

"Apolonia, we have been over and over this," Don Vega said, his voice ringing with frustration.

"No, we haven't, Father. Tell him, Mr. LaMont."

"I beg your pardon?"

"Tell him about Stoddard."

"What about Stoddard?" Don Vega said, and Gideon and Clint began to worry.

"He took my honor."

"What?" her father roared.

"It is true," Apolonia said, relief in her voice. "Tell him, Mr. LaMont."

Don Vega stared into Gideon's dark face, his look pleading for reassurance that it wasn't so.

"I don't know," Gideon said truthfully.

"And just what do you think he was doing, Mr. LaMont?" Apolonia asked.

"Well, it was dark, and I couldn't see real well."

Clint could have sworn Gideon was beginning to blush, but Clint was beginning to see what Apolonia was trying to accomplish, and he decided to help her.

"He was surely in a position —"

"*Mi Dios!*" Don Vega looked crestfallen. "The Cota family will never allow it."

"But we don't have to let anyone know, Father." Apolonia laid a hand on her father's arm, placating him with her soft voice. "Just tell the Cotas that the wedding is off."

"If they don't have to know . . ." His voice rang with hope. "Surely you women have ways . . . ways to fool a man." He glanced at Clint and Gideon. It was his turn to color.

"I would not know, Father. But this woman will tell the Cotas, if you attempt to force this wedding."

Don Vega dismounted from the rail, his head hanging. He made his way to the hacienda, Clint, Gideon, and Apolonia staring after him.

"He'll get over it," she finally said.

"Stoddard didn't really . . . he didn't . . ." Gideon's jaw tightened at the thought that he hadn't been in time to prevent Stoddard from having his way.

Apolonia flashed him a sly grin, winked at him, and with ladylike grace walked after her father.

"I'll never understand women," Clint said.

"I'm not sure I want to."

They readjusted their positions on the top rail and looked over the small herd of horses.

"I'm gonna need some help driving these animals to Sonora. How about coming along?" Clint asked.

Gideon tipped his top hat. "I believe I've taken to the city life." That drew a smile from Clint.

"Hasn't it been about long enough for the LaMonts to have gotten your letter, and couldn't they be on their way to San Francisco by now? How many of them did you say there were?"

"Henri had two brothers and an uncle with four grown sons." Gideon arched an eyebrow, beginning to see what Clint was driving at.

"All duelers and dead shots, I believe you said."

"You're cagey as those cotton-pickin' women, Clint Ryan."

"If you don't want to risk being back pickin' cotton, maybe you'd like a job driving horses. Doesn't pay much, but it beats gettin' beat." Clint jumped off the rail into the corral.

"I'll have you know I held a position in the stable caring for the family's best stock. Then I became Henri LaMont's personal man." Gideon's look changed to one of compliance. "Maybe a little time in the gold country wouldn't be so bad after all." Gideon tipped his high hat again. "Think I can trade this for a sombrero?"

"Pick yourself out a cayuse, cowhand." Clint laughed and shook out his reata.